Murder Most English

*

The Lady Jane & Mrs Forbes Mysteries

Book One

B. D. CHURSTON

ISBN: 9798373071376

One

A thought struck Kate Forbes. What might it be like to freeze to death on a mountainside? Certainly, driving through the snow-dusted southern edge of England's South Downs four days before Christmas made her wonder. Would it start with her hands?

Possibly not as she was wearing thick gloves.

Her feet then?

Yes, they were fast becoming blocks of ice.

"I hope this weather doesn't finish us off," she said from beneath a woollen muffler. "We'll freeze if we don't get to Linton Hall soon."

"I love mornings like this," came the reply from her equally well-wrapped niece, Lady Jane Scott. "Look at that sky."

1

Kate glanced up at the clear, blue heavens.

"I'd hate to suffer like they do on Mount Everest," she said as she steered left at a junction.

Jane stifled a laugh. "That's in the Himalayas, not Sussex."

"Yes, well…" Kate had to stifle a laugh too, before resolutely muttering something about wishing Gertie had proper heating – Gertie being a 1926 cherry red two-seater Austin Seven Chummy with a mischievous liking for playing dead on cold mornings.

"She's doing well," said Jane.

"Gertie? I get the feeling she prefers summertime."

"Ah, she likes to show off with her roof folded back, does she?"

"Yes, she does, and who can blame her!"

As they rumbled down a country lane, Kate's thoughts turned from the perils of winter driving to her niece's future. Twenty-six-year-old Lady Jane was the daughter of Robert Scott, the Earl of Oxley, who had done very well in business. Jane had recently broken off her engagement to a viscount from the Midlands, so might she find Edward, heir to the Linton estate, more to her liking? Or should Kate have kept out of it and refused Lord Linton's request to have Jane introduced to his son?

It was difficult to know.

But such thoughts took flight as, just yards ahead, a bright blue traction engine emerged unexpectedly from an open side gate.

"Auntie!"

Kate swerved across the lane, halfway into the tangle of barren hedgerow, and around the trundling mechanical menace.

Thankfully, any urge to give the engine driver a piece of her mind was disarmed by his friendly wave.

"According to the map, it's not far now," said Jane once they were back on track.

As if to oblige, the hedgerows on their right soon tapered off to give a view across a shallow vale of bone hard fields. High on the far side stood Linton Hall with its Portland stone façade bathed in winter sunshine.

"At last," said Kate with relief in her voice.

"It looks quite old," said Jane.

"It is. The first Baron Linton bought it from the Clarendon family in 1768. The fifth baron had the interior modified, or some say ruined, in the 1850s."

"You know the Lintons' history well."

"I've spent many an evening there. Rest assured, Lord Linton will be only too happy to enlighten you further."

"Ooh, any scandals or grisly murders in the annals?"

"Oh… one or two."

"Really?"

"Oh, a long time ago! But enough about murderous misdeeds. I'm looking forward to us catching up with each other's news."

"Me too. It's been a while."

Beneath her muffler, Kate smiled. She had frequently seen her niece between the ages of fourteen and eighteen, when Jane attended the Roedean School for girls, not far from Kate's home on the coast. That came to an end though when Jane went up to Somerville College, Oxford and later sought work as a researcher. Their encounters since had been few and far between. A situation unlikely to change much going forward.

"Ah, I'd better start braking…"

Kate held her foot down firmly as Gertie's downhill trajectory meant she was threatening to top thirty-five miles an hour.

It wasn't much of a hill though and it soon bottomed out at the village of Wensford and the River Arun, which they crossed by way of a picturesque three-arch stone bridge. Despite the cold, there were a few people dotted about: two men by the Red Lion pub here, a herdsman with some cows outside a shed there. No doubt most were indoors, engaged in everything from darning socks through to pickling onions. In the grip of winter, life in the countryside continued.

Before long, they were across the valley and approaching open iron gates set into a stone wall. Barely slowing, Kate drove straight through onto a long drive fringed with trees and large shrubs, some of them evergreen to counter an otherwise barren winter vista.

"What a glorious estate," said Jane. "Is it good for walking?"

"Yes, especially in summer."

"I'm sure winter walks are lovely too, Aunt."

As they neared the Lintons' home, they got a much better view. And an impressive sight it was too, with an imposing pediment over the central windows and front door. The overall effect was one of grandeur, permanence, and wealth.

"Do they have a library?" Jane asked.

"Yes, but it's not much of a collection. George is a hoarder of random things. It's not all books either."

"Oh…" Jane sounded disappointed.

"He has guns in there… ceremonial swords and daggers… large vases… all sorts. He just buys things he takes a liking to. He's lovely though – someone who enjoys life and wants others to enjoy it too."

Kate was looking forward to seeing the Lintons again. It had been three years, the longest time apart from her friend Florence Nettleton, sister of Lord Linton's late wife, Rose. Their reunion would be full of joy and, no doubt, gossip.

"Well, here we are," she said as Gertie came to a halt on the crunchy gravel. "It'll be fun. And that's just what we need. George really is the perfect host. Oh, the parties we had in the old days."

For a moment, she was drawn back to the years before the War, when the world had seemed so full of happiness and hope. The early 1920s had seen a return of that spirit, although it didn't last. But there was little point in lamenting the past. George, the seventh baron, was a cheery old thing, and thankfully, that was also true of his son, Oliver, whose twenty-fifth birthday they would be celebrating tomorrow.

Just then, a fresh-faced young footman hurried out of the house to open Kate's door. Jane meanwhile was already out of the car and stretching her legs. Following the footman in a more measured fashion, Pritchard the greying, somewhat portly butler addressed them.

"Good morning, Mrs Forbes. Good morning, Lady Jane."

Kate smiled. "Pritchard! Three years and you haven't changed a bit. I trust Lord Linton is well?"

"Alas, no, Mrs Forbes. I regret to inform you that his lordship is dead."

For a moment, Kate assumed she had misheard. She was expecting a reply of "his lordship is well," or "on fine form," or even "in the pink."

But dead?

Two

Without further delay, Pritchard left the footman to deal with the luggage while he showed the ladies into the warmth of the oak-panelled entrance hall, which the Lintons referred to as the foyer.

It was an unquestionably grand space, with a high ceiling, a wide oak staircase, elaborate plasterwork, stylish Italian chandeliers, gilt-framed mirrors and imposing portraits in oils – while, over the fireplace, an oak shield bore the family's coat of arms and Latin motto, *vires in unitate*.

In fact, so full of objects was the foyer, it was easy to overlook the fine craftsmanship of the Queen Anne side table half covered with a green cloth and ornaments, the exquisite Victorian grandfather clock that chimed hourly from an alcove by the front door, and an extraordinary wrought iron frame in the shape of a leaping lion, currently in use as an umbrella stand.

Having handed their hats and coats to Pritchard, Kate glanced up at the portrait of the third baron: a mean-looking, sallow-faced man with a walrus moustache. She then translated the family motto: strength in unity. Despite the passing of Lord Linton, the family would undoubtedly pull together.

Next, she tidied her hair in a mirror.

"You're looking marvellous, Aunt," said Jane.

"Thank you. Although these days there's the mystery of extra grey upstairs and extra pounds down below. I've no idea how they get there."

Finally, she gazed upon Pritchard's resolute visage.

"Poor old George," she uttered.

"Yes, madam. The police and Dr Renfrew should be here soon."

"The police? I see…"

Of course, Kate was used to events involving the police. Her recently departed husband, Henry, had been a judge who often recounted courtroom tales across the dinner table. But what of poor Jane? She glanced at her niece, whose short auburn hair was tucked stylishly behind her ears, and whose warm brown eyes and friendly smile belied a sharp, intelligent and meticulous mind.

"How are Edward, Oliver and Charlotte?" Jane asked, clearly managing admirably.

"They're coping as best they can, Lady Jane," Pritchard replied stoically.

"Kate! Jane!"

They both looked beyond Pritchard to a thin, silver-haired woman dressed in purple and black entering the foyer from the hallway.

"Florrie!" cried Kate. "What a shock. Poor old George…"

"Yes, poor old George," her old friend Florence Nettleton echoed as she joined them. "And Jane, I haven't seen you since you were tiny."

Jane smiled. "They say time flies."

"It does," said Florence. "Now, obviously Oliver's party's off. Most of the young ones are going home, although a few close to the Lintons are staying on for a bit. Some have travelled a fair distance."

"As have we," said Kate, referring to a twenty-mile drive that had taken an hour and a quarter to complete.

"Oh, absolutely," said Florence. "You must be exhausted."

"Would you like some refreshment?" Pritchard enquired, having deposited their coats in the cloakroom. "Perhaps some hot tea in the morning room?"

"We might rest after our journey," said Kate. "Could we have tea in our rooms?"

"Of course, madam," he replied before disappearing into the hallway.

"Oh Kate," said Florence, "how are you keeping? It's barely six months since poor Henry…"

"Yes, six months. Still, we do our best."

Although, doing her best hadn't been easy for Kate.

"So," she said. "Do we know how George died?"

"I'm sure it was quite natural. His heart had been deteriorating over the past year or two. Very similar to my dear Richard some years back."

"Ah, poor Richard. Such a fine husband, Florrie."

"Yes, he was."

"Ladies!" greeted an engaging voice approaching from the hallway.

Kate and Jane turned to face a casually dressed young man with short, wavy brown hair and a friendly smile.

"It's lovely to see you, Oliver," said Kate. "You have my sincere condolences."

"Thanks, Mrs Forbes."

"How are you all coping?"

"Charlotte's upset. Edward's in his rooms."

"May you all find some peace, Oliver."

"Thank you."

"Now, let me to introduce my niece, Lady Jane Scott."

Oliver nodded. "Lady Jane, welcome to Linton Hall."

"Thank you, Mr Linton. May I too offer my condolences."

"Thanks, and please call me Oliver. I trust you ladies weren't too cold on the way here?"

"Oh, just a slight chill," said Kate. "I don't like to complain though."

She noticed Jane's sidelong glance.

"Well, there are fires in all rooms to warm you up," said Oliver.

"Marvellous," said Kate.

She understood the Linton method. Half the house would be closed off over the winter, except when guests were staying. Then extra coal would be brought in, fires lit, and the whole house would be toasty warm for a few days. A boon for guests as well as for the Lintons' reputation as a wealthy family.

"Florrie says some of the party guests are staying on," said Kate.

"Some have come a long way," said Oliver as the footman brought in the last of their luggage.. "I hope you're not thinking of heading off too soon. Your rooms have been prepared."

"My dear Oliver," Kate boomed, "of course we'll stay. It's time to rally round!"

Oliver smiled. "Right, Croft here will take your luggage up and put your car in the garage. How about I get the maid to bring you some refreshment?"

"Pritchard's already on the case," said Kate.

"Of course."

"Ahem…"

The company turned to an apple-cheeked young man wearing a two-piece tweed suit and rimless spectacles coming from the hallway.

"Ah," said Oliver. "This is Bartholomew Grantley, a second cousin of mine on father's side. Barty, this is Mrs Kate Forbes and her niece, Lady Jane Scott."

"A pleasure to meet you, Mrs Forbes… Lady Jane," said an eager Bartholomew in a less than confident voice. "My side of the family hails from Norfolk. I'll be staying on to represent them at Lord Linton's service."

"It's very much appreciated," said Oliver.

"His lordship will be sorely missed," said Bartholomew. "He was an example to us all."

"Ha! The opposite of Edward, who now inherits the title," said a fellow coming in from the hallway.

"Oh really…" Bartholomew huffed.

"Allow me to introduce Timothy Lawson," said Oliver, his earlier cheer dissipating with the arrival of this self-assured, handsome, dark-haired man in a smart tan suit.

While Kate smiled, she wasn't impressed.

Following the introductions, Oliver continued.

"Timothy was in the same regiment as Edward during the War. These days, he's a stockbroker at Hatchborne's in the City."

"Yes," said Timothy, "and Oliver works under me there, don't you, Ollie."

"Timothy's guiding me until I find my feet," said Oliver.

"It's not all work and no play though, is it."

"No, we have a few days off now. A short run up to Christmas then back to work on Monday."

But Kate's gaze remained on Timothy.

"About Edward," she said. "You don't approve of him?"

"Well, let's face it, he hasn't welcomed a single guest."

"Perhaps he's overcome with grief," Kate suggested. Her own grief had only recently begun to wane, and still had the power to flare up unexpectedly.

But Timothy harrumphed.

"Mark my words, Edward will be the ruin of his family. And I speak from a professional standpoint – as the family's advisor on financial matters. Frankly, I fear he's on the verge of announcing some reckless new enterprise."

"I see," said Kate. "Well, if you'll excuse us, we'll make our way up to our rooms. It's been a tiring morning."

"Of course," said Oliver. "Turn right on the middle landing and it's the last two rooms on the left. Lady Jane's is the farthest. I look forward to seeing you both later."

Kate and Jane thanked him and mounted the stairs, although Kate was still troubled by Timothy Lawson's view of Edward.

There were two turns before they reached the middle landing. To the left, a wide passage gave access to the family's rooms. Kate and Jane turned right into the passage that led to the guests' rooms.

Reaching her door, Kate paused.

"Jane, come in a moment."

Jane followed her aunt into an expansive, bright room with yellow walls, white blankets over a bed almost lost against the far wall, a wardrobe, a chest of drawers, and a breakfast table with two wooden chairs. While the sun had yet to come around, the large sash window gave a lovely view over the vast formal garden at the rear of the house.

"It's a lovely room," said Jane. "So spacious."

"All the guests' rooms are," said Kate. "The family's quarters are even bigger."

"The fire's nice too. You'll be warm in here."

"Jane… there's a reason for bringing you to Linton Hall. One I've kept from you."

"You mean to meet Edward?"

"Oh. How did you know?"

"You mentioned him four times on the way here. Oliver and Charlotte only got one mention apiece."

"Yes, well, the truth is I haven't seen Edward since before the War."

"When he was a charming young man?"

"No, he was insufferable. Of course, much of that I put down to him being seventeen at the time."

"And now he's thirty-one?"

Kate sat down on the edge of the bed.

"Perhaps that chap downstairs was wrong. Perhaps Edward's matured into a fine, responsible man and all this disapproval is out of proportion."

"Possibly."

"Yes, well… you get along to your room, Jane. You must be worn out."

"What about our tea?"

"I'll just have a quick sip and close my eyes for ten minutes. If you don't mind."

"No, of course not, Aunt. I'll leave you in peace."

As Jane opened the solid oak door to leave, Oliver's voice boomed from somewhere near the stairs.

"Pritchard, where's my brother?" he demanded.

"His lordship prefers to remain in his rooms, sir."

"He's meant to be head of the family!" Oliver insisted.

Kate smiled as best she could. It really was none of their business.

Three

Following a ten-minute nap on Kate's part which lasted its customary three-quarters of an hour, the combined forces of aunt and niece came down to the large living room.

The room itself was impressive, with twin chandeliers, a brand-new radio set and naturalistic wildlife themed paintings – apart from one which, to Kate, looked like a child's portrayal of a red piano surrounded by a swirl of oranges and blues. Moreover, the usual centrepiece of a Robert Adam fireplace was somewhat overshadowed by a towering Christmas tree decorated with shiny baubles of silver and gold, and small brightly painted wooden decorations, such as a deer, a sleigh, and a jolly Father Christmas.

Meanwhile, on one of three sumptuous floral sofas were seated Florence and a brown-haired, pretty young woman wearing a knitted crimson cardigan over a pink blouse and burgundy skirt.

"Kate, Jane," said Florence, "allow me to introduce my niece on my late husband's side, Margaret Tavistock. Margaret, this is my very good friend Mrs Kate Forbes and her niece, Lady Jane Scott."

"How do you do, Margaret," said Kate.

"I'm very well, thank you, Mrs Forbes," said Margaret in a soft musical voice.

Once the introductions had been completed, and all four were seated, Florence turned to Jane.

"Margaret's a talented pianist. She gives lessons as a private music tutor, you know."

"How wonderful," said Kate.

"It's mostly wasted," said Florence. "Lots of listless children with sausage fingers."

"You never know," said Jane. "The next Liszt might be among them."

Margaret smiled.

"That would be nice."

"She's staying with me for Christmas," said Florence. "Although her early arrival was for Oliver's party."

"Alas," said Kate.

"George was so looking forward to it and to having guests for Christmas dinner too."

"Good old George," said Kate. "He'll be missed."

Florence eyed Jane.

"Mind you, it's not like the old days when he and Rose hosted parties."

"Yes, Aunt Kate mentioned it on the way here," said Jane. "Those must have been wonderful times."

"They were, but times change," said Florence.

"Indeed, they do," said Kate. "I was recently invited to something called a bring-a-bottle party."

"How dreadful," said Florence.

"Well…" Kate had found it an enjoyable, unfussy evening.

"George wouldn't have stooped so low," said Florence. "Mind you, he stopped cutting loose after my sister died. The old place definitely became quieter."

"It became quieter before then," Kate reminded her. "With Alistair's passing."

"Yes, of course," agreed Florence, turning somewhat solemn. "George's eldest son was taken by Spanish flu in 1919. Imagine surviving years of war only to succumb to illness."

"It took my mother too," said Jane. "The same year."

"Yes…" Florence sighed. "Kate mentioned it in a letter at the time. So tragic…"

With Jane's mother, Annette, being Kate's younger sister, all three women fell silent. For Kate, it was another reminder of her deepest wish to help Jane in any way she could. Not as a substitute mother, but perhaps as the best aunt possible. If only there were some kind of guidebook on that…

However, approaching voices curtailed any lengthy reflection.

A moment later, two young ladies entered.

Twenty-three-year-old Charlotte, daughter of Lord George Linton, sported cropped brunette hair and a plain form of clothing Kate could only think of as impoverished Bohemian. In contrast, her slightly older companion had a stylish Dutch bob haircut and was dressed perfectly in a deep blue tweed twin set and pearl necklace.

"Charlotte," Kate exclaimed. "How lovely to see you. I'm so sorry to come at such an awful time. You have my sincere condolences."

"Thanks, Mrs Forbes. Rest assured, it's always good to see you. I hope the journey wasn't too cold."

"Oh, I barely noticed."

Once again, Jane looked askance at her aunt.

"But look at you, Charlotte," said Kate. "A new style, perhaps?"

"Yes, I've found my spirit self."

Kate was far from convinced.

"Good for you," she said. "Now, who's your friend?"

"Let me introduce Victoria Eustace."

"A pleasure to meet you, Miss Eustace."

"And you, Mrs Forbes."

Kate half-turned to her own companion. "This is my niece, Lady Jane Scott."

They exchanged greetings and then the new arrivals joined them on the sofas.

"Any sign of Edward?" Kate wondered.

"He's in the library doing some research," said Charlotte. "He doesn't like to be disturbed."

"Oh," said Kate.

Charlotte shrugged. "Edward leads his own life, unbound by tradition."

"Hmm," said Kate. "And what about you, Miss Eustace? Are you an advocate for change?"

Victoria took a moment to consider her response.

"Tradition is something we can't estimate until it's gone. Perhaps it's a glue that holds things together. I'm no expert, but I find constant change unappealing. Oh, and by the way, please call me Victoria."

There was a knock on the open door. It was Pritchard.

"Mrs Nettleton, Miss Charlotte. The police and Dr Renfrew have arrived. I've advised his lordship and Mr Oliver. I thought you would want to know."

"Thank you, Pritchard," said Florence. "I trust we'll be informed of any developments."

Pritchard nodded and withdrew.

Charlotte huffed.

"Do the police really need to be here?"

Kate found the comment odd.

"Your father was one of the county's most important men. That said, I'm sure it's just a formality."

Just then, Timothy Lawson came in accompanied by a man of around sixty with a slight stoop.

"Sir Charles!" Kate exclaimed. "How are you?"

"All the better for seeing you, my dear," came the reply in a friendly but gravelly voice.

As always, Sir Charles Sutton looked dapper, if somewhat Victorian. Kate knew his suits were made by a tailor in Savile Row, London, with strict instructions to not wander from a design he came across in 1890. The same went for his shirt collars.

Kate introduced Jane and explained that Sir Charles was one of the departed Lord Linton's closest friends.

"We were wondering about Edward," Kate went on. "He seems to have locked himself away in the library."

Before Sir Charles could respond, Timothy butted in.

"I saw him briefly. If you ask me, the new Lord Linton looks far too pleased with himself. Honestly, I wouldn't have been surprised had his father cut him off."

Kate didn't like such talk, particularly at a time of mourning, but any response was prevented by Pritchard knocking again.

"Mrs Nettleton, Cook's prepared a cold meat buffet lunch for everyone."

"I trust it's not that beef again," Sir Charles muttered. "Tough as old boots."

"Leftovers have to be made to last," said Florence.

Kate was only too aware of it. Up and down England, death duties and taxes were hollowing out the financial wherewithal of the upper classes. Nowadays they were caught in a trap of balancing a long-standing loathing of new money with a need of funds. Jane's family had bucked the trend though. Her father had made a name for himself in manufacturing. Jane was therefore much sought after by those not so keen on eating leftovers.

*

Twenty minutes later, with the conversation focused on past festive periods, Oliver came in followed by Bartholomew Grantley.

"Dr Renfrew and the police have departed," said Oliver. "My father passed away from his heart condition. So… there we are."

"He'll be sorely missed," said Kate.

"There'll be a private family service in a couple of days," Oliver continued. "You're all very welcome to stay on."

"Absolutely," said Bartholomew, a little too keenly. "I'll be here to pay my respects."

"As will I," said Timothy Lawson, unimpressed by Bartholomew's eagerness.

"Me too," said Sir Charles, nodding in agreement.

"Now, how about a change of scenery after lunch?" Timothy suggested. "A spot of shooting."

Oliver puffed out his cheeks, perhaps sensing this wasn't a time for casual pastimes. But then his mood lightened.

"Yes, why not. Father loved shooting. Barty? Sir Charles? Fancy a pop at some clays?"

"Yes, alright," said Bartholomew, although his heart didn't appear to be in it.

"Not me, old chap," said Sir Charles. "But what about Edward? Shouldn't he be here running the show?"

"I'm sure he'll join us as soon as he can," said Oliver.

"Most gracious of him," said Sir Charles, somewhat insincerely.

As Oliver departed, Kate could only wonder about the Lintons' motto. Strength in unity? The family was falling apart.

Four

Forty-five minutes before dinner, Kate, attired in a dark blue evening dress and grey cardigan, was at her bedroom window. Not that she could see much of the garden in the winter darkness.

Her thoughts were on Edward Linton. An afternoon of tea and chatter had passed without sight of him, but surely this evening, for the sake of the family, he'd be at the dinner table.

She sat down on the edge of the bed and, for a second time, tried to pull on her new shoes. Annoyingly, they still refused to co-operate. Had her feet swollen a little?

There was a light knock at the door.

"Aunt Kate?"

"Come in, Jane. I'm almost ready."

Jane entered and closed the door behind her. She looked resplendent in a burgundy evening dress.

"You look glorious, Jane. Good enough to eat, as my grandmother used to say. Although, I'm not sure why she said it; she mainly ate pickled pork and raw eggs."

"I think the first gong's about to—" But Jane was cut short by exactly that.

"Sooner than I thought," said Kate. "Why don't you go down. I'm not sure about these shoes."

"Alright, I'll see you downstairs. Hopefully, we'll finally get to meet Edward."

However, Kate had more to say.

"George never really got over the loss of his eldest son. He thought the world of Alistair."

"Life's not always fair," said Jane, sympathetically.

Kate thought for a moment.

"What about Mr Lawson's suggestion – that Edward might announce a new enterprise. Perhaps it's a way forward for the family."

"Mr Lawson described it as reckless."

"He could be wrong."

"True."

There was a light tapping at the door.

"Kate? It's Florrie. I thought I'd come and collect you."

Jane opened the door.

"A slight delay. Aunt Kate's fussing over her shoes."

"Nonsense," said Kate, struggling to fit one of them. "We were actually discussing a certain chap's plans for a bright future. Perhaps tonight, all will be revealed with an announcement."

Florence, framed in the open doorway, was a picture of shock.

"I doubt Oliver will make his announcement tonight. Not with his father's passing. A month or two, perhaps."

"Oliver? I was referring to Edward."

"Oh."

Kate looked up at Florence, whose face had turned red, and to Charlotte Linton, Margaret Tavistock and Victoria Eustace, who were gathered behind her.

"Why don't you all go down," Kate suggested. "My footwear appears to have shrunk on the journey."

Florence duly led Jane and the others away, along the landing to the stairs.

Kate meanwhile sought more comfortable shoes. Not as stylish as those she had initially chosen, but a pair she could walk in.

A few minutes later, she set off.

Before she got to the stairs though, she spotted Pritchard at an open door along the opposite landing. She had a fair idea it was Edward's room.

"Tartan, sir," Pritchard announced, which seemed an odd thing to say.

Kate meanwhile went downstairs to join the ladies in the red drawing room. Here, two sofas of patterned red and pink woven fabric faced each other either side of a carved oak fireplace. Kate plonked herself down next to Florence and Jane, while Charlotte, Margaret and Victoria were seated opposite. Between them, on an oriental rug, stood an elegant yew table. Here, Gloria the maid served them with gin cocktails or, in Kate's case, a small dry sherry.

"Such well turned-out young ladies," said Florence.

"Yes," said Kate. "Lovely earrings, Victoria."

"They were my grandmother's."

All turned to admire the silver and sapphire teardrops.

"They're beautiful," said Jane, "and they match your dress. Where did you get it?"

Victoria was wearing a sapphire blue satin evening gown.

"I paid a visit to Barker's of Kensington," she said. "They hold fashion shows there. Exclusive Paris haute couture. Chanel, Molyneux, Lanvin, Lelong and others. It's incredibly expensive, but it really opens one's eyes."

Kate turned to Charlotte who wore a plain brown dress and string of unappealing blue wooden beads around her neck.

"Lovely beads, Charlotte."

"Thanks, Mrs Forbes," said Charlotte, stubbing her cigarette out in an ashtray. "They represent tranquillity."

"Do they? How interesting."

"May I ask a question, Mrs Forbes?" said Margaret. "I understand from my aunt that you often visited Linton Hall as a child."

"That's right, along with my sister, Annette. Our father was a lifelong friend of George's father, so we came over occasionally, especially during the summer. I remember playing with Annette and George in the garden. We were usually pirates or explorers. He was an only child, you know. Goodness me, it was such a long time ago."

"They say the house is haunted," said Margaret.

"Ah now, I can help you there," said Kate. "Every house over a hundred years old is said to be haunted. It's a well-known fact."

"That they're haunted?"

"No, the saying so."

Victoria chimed in. "I'd like to ask Lady Jane about archaeology. Mrs Nettleton tells me it's an interest of yours?"

"Yes, absolutely," said Jane. "At Oxford, Professor Peregrine Nash got a few of us interested in the subject. He's now based in Sussex, so when I get the chance, I go along to various local digs. I was at a new site a few months ago. A Saxon settlement not far from Lewes."

"Archaeology, eh?" said Sir Charles, entering the room. "Dug up any bodies lately?"

"Really, Charles," Florence protested.

"Oh, don't mind me. You know George and I shared a gallows sense of humour."

"I have to admit I'm not a wholly dedicated digger," said Jane. "Research is my main interest. I work as much as I can within academia, studying the Normans through to the Elizabethans."

"It sounds fascinating," said Margaret.

"I'm sure I could spend my entire life gaining a deeper understanding of those periods."

"A woman as professor of history?" said Victoria. "That's not likely."

"It's rare, but there *are* a few professors around who aren't men," said Jane. "It's by no means an easy path, but that won't stop me."

"I love history," said Florence. "They say it's all around us."

"It is," said Jane. "I expect even here, Linton Hall succeeded an earlier building."

"Tudor," said Sir Charles, taking a seat in the corner. "George told me there was a grotty old manor house with a large hall and damp walls. The Clarendon family had this place built. I, for one, think it's an improvement."

"It's the same in Sandham-on-Sea," said Kate. "We have some lovely Victorian Gothic houses that replaced earlier dwellings."

"I wonder if Edward will be at dinner?" Florence said, somewhat at odds with the mood.

"I'm sure he'll come down to see everyone," said Charlotte.

"He's the eighth baron," said Victoria. "I dare say the family's had a range of personalities at the helm."

"Humph," Sir Charles grunted.

"He's not so bad," said Charlotte. "He worked hard in Paris to find his place in life." She turned to Jane. "He got involved in the art scene as a dealer after the War."

"Yes, Aunt Kate told me about it on the journey here. She said Edward came back to England three months ago."

"Which is why I haven't seen him in such a long time," said Kate. "I've watched you and Oliver growing up, but I haven't set eyes on Edward since he was seventeen. Still, I'm sure he'll be a worthy head of the family."

"I hope so," said Florence. "Some of us relied on George's generosity."

"Money isn't everything," said Charlotte.

Kate was tempted to reprimand someone who had plenty of the stuff, but Bartholomew Grantley and Timothy Lawson came in, sparking a round of greetings and gin slings.

Bartholomew in particular was in a good mood, prompting Kate to ask him how things were going.

"Marvellous, Mrs Forbes," he responded. "Couldn't be better. In fact, I'd go as far to say there are exciting times ahead."

"Good for you. I like to hear of young people getting on. How about you, Mr Lawson?"

"Things aren't too bad. I have to say I find this whole business with Edward rather infuriating though. This won't go well for him."

"Yes, well, the second gong can't be far off," said Sir Charles. "I dare say we'll soon learn the new baron's thoughts on his role."

Five

The dining room at Linton Hall boasted a marble fireplace, mahogany furniture and sea green walls that set off the gilt frames of various rural idyll paintings.

Eleven places had been laid for dinner. Ten of those were now occupied – the exception being at the head of the table.

From the opposite end, Sir Charles Sutton was among the most voluble of those expressing concern that this was most irregular.

Seated immediately to the right of the head of the table, Oliver Linton concurred.

"I'll go and get him if I have to."

Also on Oliver's side were Jane, Timothy Lawson and Victoria Eustace, while facing him were Kate, Florence, Charlotte, Bartholomew Grantley and, closest to Sir Charles, Margaret Tavistock.

"Perhaps the gong doesn't travel to all parts of the house," said Kate, despite the instrument being centrally placed in the foyer between the stairs and the hallway.

"He'll be down," Charlotte reassured them. "Let's not draw conclusions when we've only just taken our seats."

As if on cue, Pritchard entered.

"Ladies and gentlemen, his lordship will join you now."

The gathering collectively held its breath as Edward, dressed in a garish green suit, strode in holding a glass of brandy. Without a word, he took his seat.

"Long live Lord Linton," said Bartholomew, raising his glass of claret.

A few of those at the table looked at Bartholomew with incredulity, but Edward seemed happy enough, raising his glass to his advocate.

He was much as Kate remembered. Tall, dark, and handsome although a little fuller in the face, and now sporting a moustache. She wondered. Had he matured somewhat? Or was he the same demanding, selfish egotist.

"Mrs Forbes," he finally declared as if he'd only just noticed her. "What a pleasure. It's been a long time."

She'd forgotten the calculating tone of his voice.

"I trust your lordship is well?" she asked.

"I am. And I see you've brought a companion."

"Yes, may I introduce my niece, Lady Jane Scott."

"The daughter of the admirable Earl of Oxley, no less. It's good to meet you, Lady Jane. I hope you enjoy your stay with us."

"Thank you, Lord Linton. It's a lovely house."

"Please call me Edward. It's much more sociable."

"As you wish, Edward."

Kate wasn't at all convinced. Edward Linton had the charm of a cobra. Introducing Jane was meant to be a possible prelude to matrimony, but this was clearly the same old Edward.

"So, what do you get up to, Lady Jane?" he asked.

Kate cut in. "Nothing of interest. She's quite a dull girl, really."

"I have my moments," said Jane.

"I'm sure you do," said Edward.

Oliver sighed. "You've taken father's place. Would you like to say a few words?"

"A few words? Well, brother, only to let you all know that I intend to make a fresh start. Whatever happened in the past should remain there. We live in a time of forward thinking."

"Yes, we do," said Charlotte.

"I meant a few words about father," Oliver prompted.

"We'll miss him," said Edward. "Now, Pritchard, where's the soup?"

Pritchard signalled to Gloria and soon those seated were being served French onion soup from a large tureen.

"So, Lady Jane?" said Bartholomew from along the table. "Do you travel much? I'm a regular visitor to Paris. Been going for years. I wonder if you're familiar with it?"

"No, but I'm sure I'll go one day."

"Charlotte and I were in Paris during the summer," said Victoria. "We had fun, didn't we."

"Yes, I suppose we did," said Charlotte.

"Paris is dreary," rumbled Timothy. "I was recently in Monte Carlo. It's so invigorating, especially if you like boats and warm seas. Ideal for swimming."

"It's another place I look forward to visiting at some point," said Jane.

"Are you not a traveller?" asked Margaret from across the table.

"I've travelled a little. Vienna, Rome and Athens. And I've visited Egypt to see the Pyramids."

"The Pyramids," Margaret gasped. "That sounds exciting."

"I went with my friend Anna Finch and her parents. Rome and Athens was a trip with my father, while I visited Vienna on my own last year."

"How interesting," said Bartholomew. "I'd love to visit Egypt, and Italy and Greece, and Vienna!"

"How predictable," said Timothy. "Why don't you just ask Lady Jane about her rich father."

"Is anyone here a fellow angler?" Oliver asked, rapidly changing the subject.

Bartholomew jumped in. "Oh yes, me."

"The weather's crisp and clear. I might try a spot of fishing tomorrow after lunch. Care to join me?"

"Oh… tomorrow?" Bartholomew backed away by spooning some soup into his mouth.

Edward laughed. "A tad too chilly for you, old boy?"

Timothy laughed too.

Unsurprisingly, Bartholomew leapt back in.

"I was out shooting this afternoon, wasn't I? No, I'm in for some fishing. If you have some spare tackle, Oliver, I'll be right by your side."

"How about a wager on the catch," said Timothy. "My money's on Ollie for the most fish. Barty, the only thing you'll catch is a cold."

"You don't know that."

"Hmm, here's another wager for you, Barty," said Edward. "One you might win. Your jacket lining. Is it blue? Is it red? Let me have a guess. Is a guinea alright for you?"

"A guinea? That's ridiculous."

"Too rich for your blood?"

"No, of course not. I accept."

"Tartan."

"What?"

Bartholomew opened his jacket and Edward shrugged.

"Lucky guess, old chap. Don't forget that guinea, will you."

Kate was appalled. Wasn't cheating beneath a baron? Then again, prior knowledge of Bartholomew's jacket lining wasn't as low as the third Baron Linton's acquisition of the title following the suspicious deaths of the three people ahead of him in line.

"Now," said Edward. "Is anyone else tired of the décor in this decaying old heap?"

"Perhaps now isn't the time," said Oliver. "Father was fond of the house."

"Times change."

"Try acting with a little dignity, brother. No head of the Linton family should carry on in a way that brings our reputation into question."

But Edward declined to comment, leaving a silence accentuated by the sound of people consuming their soup.

A short while later, Charlotte caught Jane's attention.

"You might be interested to know I've created some new knitting patterns."

"How lovely," said Jane. "Do you draw them yourself?"

"Yes, I pluck them from my imagination. I have over fifty now and more keep coming."

"Charlotte's very creative," said Florence. "She works with lots of colours you don't always see in the shops."

"Do you dye them yourself?" Kate asked.

"Sometimes. I have to be careful though. Some colours come from substances that aren't good for one's health."

Victoria joined in. "I've seen Charlotte's creative ideas. She's ever so talented."

"Thanks," said Charlotte. "Of course, at the moment, it's all winter woollies, scarves and mittens."

Victoria nodded. "She currently has me working on a thick, black and white Mexican poncho."

"Fascinating," said Timothy before turning to Edward. "These plans for the house. As a financial advisor, I ought to warn that even minor works can run up huge bills."

"It's really none of your business," said Edward.

"Is that so?"

"Oh, come on, you two," said Sir Charles. "You were chums in the army."

"We served in the same regiment," said Timothy. "That's all."

"Well, I think the new Lord Linton is a grand chap," said Bartholomew. "With the right support, he'll do well."

"All stick together, you mean," said Timothy with a scowl. "Lucky for you, your mother married well."

While Bartholomew looked suitably chastened, Florence piped up.

"Bartholomew has a very good business brain. He'll do well in life, I'm sure of it."

But Edward's thoughts seemed to be elsewhere.

"I'm also thinking about the grounds. The garden is too formal."

"You're certainly full of plans," said Oliver.

"Yes, I am."

This was clearly a tonic for Bartholomew, who came back to life.

"Could you tell us of any other plans you might have?"

Edward smiled. "Yes, I'm leaving England. I'm going to live and work in New York."

Bartholomew dropped his spoon, causing a clang as it hit his almost empty bowl. A spot of soup now adorned his white napkin.

"New York?" Oliver asked.

"Yes," said Edward. "As a man of means, I'll be pursuing a new venture in a new country. It's true I'll be alone, but I'm sure New York's famous hospitality will stretch to a titled man from Old England. And as for Linton Hall, I might sell it."

A degree of shock reverberated around the table.

"What about the family?" said Charlotte.

"What about the staff?" said Florence. "And myself?"

"You can't sell our home," said Oliver. "It's the backbone of the community."

"No, it's not," said Edward. "You're living in the wrong century. Fetes, charities, committees. Bah."

Sir Charles rallied. "Dear old George carried out those duties for decades. Longer than any other Linton, I'd say. To my reckoning, he held the barony for forty-seven years. And in all that time, he never wavered."

"He didn't quite hold the title the longest," said Victoria. "I studied the family tree last summer. I think you'll find the second baron held the title for forty-nine years."

"Yes," said Oliver, "although the third baron only lasted a month, so you never know."

Six

After dinner, the men remained at the table for cigars, port and brandy. The ladies meanwhile decamped to the red drawing room.

Here, Kate, Florence and Jane took to one sofa, Charlotte, Margaret and Victoria the other. Between them, on the yew table, Gloria the maid was placing silver pots of tea and coffee alongside the bone china cups and saucers that had been set out earlier.

Sipping hot drinks, the conversation was soon flowing freely.

"Did you celebrate Guy Fawkes night?" Victoria asked Kate and Jane.

"I went to a bonfire party on the beach near my home in Sandham-on-Sea," said Kate. "We had sausages and a nip of whisky." She omitted mentioning her sorrow at attending it without Henry.

"I was in London," said Jane. "There was the most spectacular fireworks display in the Crystal Palace gardens."

"Wonderful," said Margaret. "I love fireworks."

"We were at the Handforth's party in Arundel," said Victoria. "It's quite the thing to be seen there. Fireworks, a roasted side of pig, and champagne. I went with Oliver. We had such a good time."

"I was there too," said Charlotte, lighting a cigarette. "Ginny Handforth's a friend."

"Did Edward go?" Kate asked.

"No," said Florence. "He lit a small bonfire in the grounds here. George and I watched from the window."

"Lady Jane…" Margaret began. "Aunt Florence tells me there were hopes of a friendship between you and Edward."

Jane took a moment before answering.

"He's a strange one. I'm sure I'm not alone in thinking that."

"You're not," said Kate. "An introduction was something I discussed with the late Lord Linton. It was entirely informal."

Florence grinned. "Well, that certainly gives young Barty a flying start."

Glances were exchanged, although Jane could only frown.

"Bartholomew Grantley… he seemed unhappy when Edward mentioned going to New York."

"It was the first I'd heard of it," said Charlotte, "but if Edward's had a spark of inspiration, then good for him."

"He said he might sell the house," Kate reminded her.

"Oh, I'm sure he won't," said Charlotte, although her words seemed to lack certainty.

"Either way, it won't be easy for you, my dear," said Florence. "Your father was a generous man. Edward is quite the opposite."

Victoria shook her head. "Charlotte isn't interested in money. She's a free spirit."

To Kate, Charlotte's acknowledging smile looked half-hearted.

"You're something of a history student, Victoria," said Jane, possibly to change the subject.

"Only in a small way. Local history, families, that sort of thing. I'm fascinated by your greater grasp though, especially your archaeological exploits."

"Well, as I said, I go on the occasional dig when I get the chance."

"Ugh, all that mud," said Florence.

"It's both fascinating and fun, Mrs Nettleton," Jane insisted. "The amazing things we can learn if only we're patient enough."

*

Half an hour later, the men joined the ladies. But Edward wasn't with them.

41

"Has our host retired?" Florence asked.

"He's gone up to his rooms," said Oliver.

"You know George had doubts," said Sir Charles. "Edward grew up as the second son. The sense of responsibility required by the head of a family doesn't always come easily."

"He's out of control," said Timothy Lawson. "A man out of control is just as likely to act on a silly whim as good advice."

"And that's the truth!" said Bartholomew, who, perhaps aided by a couple of brandies, seemed somewhat shorn of his earlier support for the new Lord Linton.

"Perhaps he'll grow into his new role over the coming months," said Kate, somewhat optimistically. "All this New York talk might be long forgotten by then."

It was a hope that failed to attract strong support.

*

Kate felt a gentle nudge.

"Eh? What?"

She opened her eyes and took the necessary few moments to grasp that she had fallen asleep on the sofa by the fire.

"Oh… it's not bedtime, is it?"

"Yes, Aunt Kate. It's almost eleven."

Apart from Jane, only Oliver, Sir Charles and Bartholomew remained.

"You go up, Jane," said Kate. "I'll be along shortly."

"I'll say goodnight then. And don't close those eyes again."

"I won't."

Giving in to a yawn, Kate also promised herself to avoid sitting too close to the fire next time.

"I trust you had a pleasant evening?" Oliver enquired.

"Very much so, thank you. I do hope you and Edward can find some common ground. It's so unfortunate when families fall out."

"Indeed."

Kate refreshed herself with a glass of water from a carafe and listened for a few minutes as the men discussed gardening, of all things.

Finally, she rose from the sofa.

"Good night then, gentlemen."

All bade her good night in return.

As Kate reached the stairs, the clock began to chime from the alcove. She smiled. The Lintons had always been a family to act on whims and urges rather than according to a timetable. Unlike the staff, of course, who ran the place like clockwork in the background.

Climbing the stairs, she wondered what tomorrow might bring. Linton Hall had been a place of constancy over such a long period. And now, it seemed that anything might happen.

"Oh well… it's really none of my business," she told herself.

Nearing the top, she heard hushed but agitated voices.

It was an argument between Timothy and Edward. Much had clearly already been said, but Timothy made a remark about the War and how 'the incident' could damage Edward.

She felt guilty for listening but was fascinated. Then, almost imperceptibly, she heard a door close on the guests' landing.

Coming back to her senses, she let out a loud cough, mounted the last few steps and turned for her room without looking the other way.

A short while later, getting ready for bed, she felt a slight breeze. Had the window been left open a crack?

She checked.

No, it was just the usual ill-fitting affair.

Getting under the covers, she thought of Jane. What discord had she brought her poor niece into? No doubt, her prayers before sleep would have to include an apology to Jane's dear late mother, along with a promise to do better.

Seven

Jane joined Kate in her room for a breakfast of coffee and porridge brought in by Gloria the maid. Sitting at the small table by the fire, they discussed the events of the previous evening – in particular, Lord Edward Linton.

"It's fair to say I don't warm to him," said Jane. "Then again, it's hard to see how anyone would get along with him."

Kate considered it.

"In the old days, a woman didn't have to like a man to marry him. I must say though, the present practice of liking the man first does have a certain attraction to it. I can see why it's caught on."

Jane laughed. "So, you wouldn't want to see me married off to Edward?"

"I only want you to be happy, Jane." And Kate meant it more than anything else in a long time.

A soft knock on the door interrupted them.

"Come in," called Kate.

"It's only me," announced Florence as she came in. "Did you have a good night's rest?"

"Yes, thanks, Florrie. We're both refreshed and looking forward to the day, whatever it may bring."

"Yes, indeed. We may learn more about Edward's plans. Then again, we might not."

"What will you do if the house is sold?" Kate asked, genuinely worried for her old friend.

"I'm not sure. Up until yesterday it wasn't something I'd ever thought about."

Kate sympathised. Being alone in the world wasn't much fun. Up until her husband's passing, life had been so simple. Now she found herself having to bolster her own confidence by being outwardly decisive, even when she often felt quite the opposite. Deep down, the real Kate was a little less certain in life, but like so many others, she had been brought up to always show fortitude.

Jane smiled at Florence. "Our thoughts have been with Edward, Oliver and Charlotte. But we're very much thinking of you too, Mrs Nettleton."

"Thank you, Lady Jane. That's very much appreciated."

"Have you seen any of the Lintons this morning?" Kate asked.

"Oliver's downstairs. He's just like his father, you know. A real chip off the old block. As for Edward, he generally keeps himself to himself for the first half of the morning."

"And Charlotte?" Jane asked.

"She's having breakfast in her room. Whatever you might think, she misses her father. He was… what shall we say… supportive?"

"Ah, the simple, bohemian lifestyle," said Kate. "It no doubt requires funds."

"George wasn't too troubled by Charlotte's choices. It'll be different with Edward though. He won't fund her. She'll have to marry."

*

After breakfast, they came down to the living room. Here, Oliver was seated by the Christmas tree with a volume of G. K. Chesterton.

He rose on seeing them.

"Good morning, ladies."

"Good morning and happy birthday, Oliver," said Kate, handing over a card.

"Yes, happy birthday," Jane echoed.

"Thanks. I trust you slept well?"

"We did," said Kate. "Yesterday was a busy day."

Oliver opened the card and found a gift inside – a green and silver bobbin lace bookmark.

"Oh, it's lovely. Thanks very much."

He then read the card which detailed a hope of good health and fortune for the recipient. It was signed by both Kate and Jane.

"Most kind," he said, placing the card on the mantlepiece beside a few others. "I'm only sorry you had to experience my brother spoiling things at dinner."

"There's no need to apologise," said Kate. "Perhaps it's this New York business. Has he said what it's about yet?"

"No, but it'll be something to do with art."

"Oh well. I must say your tree's a cheery sight."

"Yes, we had to trim a few inches off the top to make it fit."

"Can I ask about your paintings?" said Jane. "They're lovely, but that one seems at odds with the rest."

She was indicating the modernist painting of a piano.

"Edward brought it back from Paris," Oliver said rather flatly. "It's an example of expressionism he found in a studio sale."

"It's very colourful," said Kate.

"He no doubt overpaid for it," said Oliver. "Anyway, a new day awaits. I'll be down by the river after lunch enjoying a spot of fishing."

"Ah yes," said Jane. "And with Bartholomew for company. He didn't seem half as keen as you, though."

"Oh, he'll be just dandy once he's by the water. I'm sure we'll bring back something for dinner."

Kate decided that Oliver was a most suitable young man. She wondered if Jane might agree. But hadn't she decided it wasn't her role to marry off her niece? Well, obviously, if the right man presented himself…

*

Around mid-morning, wearing coats and mittens, Kate and Jane were taking the air on the terrace at the rear of the house. With the sun shining from a clear blue sky and any overnight frost long gone, Kate found the view over the large formal garden pleasing.

She was also enjoying the not-so-experienced tinkling of a piano coming from the music room, where Oliver could be seen at the keyboard.

"Would you agree he's a nice chap, Jane?"

"I would," said Jane with a light, knowing laugh. "But let's enjoy the garden, shall we?"

To the echoing ark-ark of a distant crow, they moved into the layout of twenty large squares, each no doubt diverse and beautiful in summer but muted just before Christmas. Even so, they took in the surviving white roses, the sturdier herbs, white and purple heathers, winter honeysuckle, pansies, snowdrops and many others. How spectacular it would be come June!

On the way back, they were passing the kitchen, where Cook was at the half-glass back door taking the air. No doubt a break from a hot stove or oven.

"Good morning, Cook," said Kate. She knew the woman by sight, as the rosy-cheeked servant had been with the Lintons seemingly forever.

"Good morning, madam."

Kate addressed her niece. "Jane, Mrs Parker's been here for… goodness knows how many years."

"Almost thirty, madam. When I came here, the old queen was still on the throne."

"Marvellous," said Jane. "It's so good to have long associations in life."

Through the glass, Kate spotted a large chocolate cake on the kitchen table.

"I say, that looks good."

Cook turned to see.

"The cake? It was for Mr Oliver's birthday, but he's asked for it to be served ordinarily in slices later without any fanfare."

"Yes, of course," said Kate.

"On account of his father's passing," Cook added needlessly.

"Well, I'm sure it's delicious."

"Would you like a piece?"

Kate's head shook in the negative while her mouth opened and let slip, "Just a small slice."

"And you, my lady?"

Jane shook her head. "Bless you, Cook, but no thanks."

They left soon after with Kate picking at chocolate cake from a napkin.

"There's a further connection between Cook and the Lintons," she said between mouthfuls. "Her son, Reggie, God rest his soul, was Edward's batman during the War, but he never came back. He died a hero running a top-secret message. Apologies for telling you that while I'm eating cake. Most inappropriate."

"That's alright. Unfortunately, it's one of a million such stories."

"Yes, indeed…"

As Kate reflected on loss for a moment, her gaze took in the stables. There were no horses though. George had never been interested in equestrianism, choosing instead to convert the structure into a garage wide enough for half a dozen cars. Hopefully, Gertie was getting on with the other vehicles.

A short while later, they finished their exercise and came in through the front door. With no staff on hand, they placed their coats in the cloakroom, changed their footwear, and made their way along the hallway to the right.

The blue drawing room was up ahead on the left opposite the library. Farther along, there were three more rooms: the music room on the left, the study on the right and, at the end of the corridor, the billiards room.

At the open door to the blue drawing room, they peered inside. Here, Charlotte and Margaret were being served tea by Gloria, while, in the corner by the fireplace, a radio set transmitted light orchestral music.

"Would you care to join us?" Charlotte asked.

Kate and Jane both nodded with a unified, "Yes, please."

"I'll get more cups," said Gloria before departing.

Kate sat down but jumped up again, having landed on something.

"Ah, Victoria's knitting bundle," Charlotte explained. "She was here earlier."

"Hmm," said Kate, moving the offending needles and black and white wool.

"Would you like a biscuit, Mrs Forbes?" said Margaret, proffering a tin of Huntley & Palmer's assorted creams.

"Ooh…" Kate glanced at the clock. It was half-past eleven. "It's almost lunchtime, so just a couple. I'm trying to cut down."

Just then, Oliver appeared at the door.

"Charlotte… ladies… just to confirm there'll be a private service at the church for Father tomorrow morning at ten."

Charlotte nodded.

"Such a sad affair," said Kate. "We'll be there, of course."

"It's very much appreciated. Now, I don't expect guests to travel ready to mourn, so, I'm sending young Croft and the maid to Arundel to pick up some appropriate items in black. Shawls for the ladies; ties and armbands for the men."

"That's very helpful, Oliver. Will there be many in attendance?"

"I've been in touch with the broader family and friends, so yes, our numbers should go up."

"I'm glad."

"Of course, Father loved spring, so I'm thinking we'll have a proper celebration of his life in April or May. Invite the whole village, sort of thing. Lots of hymns and flowers, and some charitable donations."

"That sounds wonderful," said Kate. "I'm sure I'll come along. I do love a good hymn."

"Me too," said Jane.

As Oliver thanked them, Edward appeared beside him. Despite looking smart in a dark blue blazer with a crisp white handkerchief in the breast pocket, his eyes were glassy, suggesting excessive drink had been consumed.

"Ladies…" he said by way of acknowledgement. He then turned to Oliver. "About tomorrow. I thought you might give the eulogy for Father."

"No, that's your job."

Edward sighed and walked away again.

Oliver turned to the ladies.

"Well, I'll be off. Things to do before lunch."

Watching him go, it struck Kate that Oliver seemed far more suited than Edward to the role of baron.

Eight

Kate and Jane were having lunch with Florence, Charlotte, Victoria and Margaret in the morning room. The fare of cold meat and bread was filling, but Kate would have preferred a steaming bowl of soup.

While they ate, Florence pondered marriage.

"Just what constitutes a suitable prospect these days? A man of means? A man with prospects?"

"A man from a good family," Victoria suggested.

"A man with a passion for art," Charlotte added.

"A man of music?" Kate asked Margaret.

Margaret blushed. "I'm not sure a shared interest is essential. Perhaps it's more important that a man has integrity."

"What do we make of Mr Lawson?" Kate wondered.

"There's a darkness to him," said Charlotte. "Have you noticed how he snaps at people when he's unhappy?"

"What about Mr Grantley?" said Victoria. "He seems a little out of place."

"Nonsense," said Kate. "He's a distant cousin of the Lintons. He also appears to have a good business brain. I'm sure he'll do well in life."

"And Edward?" Florence mused.

Victoria frowned. "He's nothing like Oliver."

Even Charlotte now seemed less certain.

"Perhaps Edward as baron is all wrong. After all, it was never in his stars."

"Yes, of course," agreed Florence. "Poor Alistair."

"What about us women?" said Jane, shifting the focus. "While keeping a home and having children is admirable, I suspect some of us also seek a place in the wider world."

"A woman can't be stifled if she marries a strong man," said Victoria. "She'll find a purpose in supporting him."

"Absolutely," said Jane. "But what if a woman such as Margaret were to marry a man who wished her to give up the piano?"

"Never marry a man who's against the arts," Charlotte advised.

"Well, it's certainly a complex field of study," said Kate. "I do wish you all happy hunting."

Jane and Margaret smiled.

"Speaking of the piano," said Florence, "I happen to know Margaret has some Mozart up her sleeve to entertain us after dinner."

"Wonderful," said Kate. "I love Mozart. Actually, now I think of it, Jane plays the piano."

"Badly," said Jane. "I once spent a winter learning Mozart's Sonata Number Sixteen without doing it justice. And remember, this is the one he wrote for beginners."

"The Sonata Facile in C major," said Margaret, coming to life. "I could help you with that. After lunch if you like."

"Are you sure? I don't have the sheet music."

"We'll manage perfectly well from memory."

"It might take a million repetitions."

"Honestly, it's no trouble at all."

*

After lunch, Kate left the morning room in search of a thicker cardigan. Reaching the hallway by the foyer, however, she heard voices from further along. It was Edward being boorish again. Then she heard Oliver telling him to behave himself.

"I'm drowning my sorrows!" Edward insisted.

"Celebrating, more like. When are you off to New York?"

"I refuse to discuss it."

Suddenly, Oliver was marching towards Kate.

"Will he be alright?" she asked.

"Oh, he'll sleep it off in the library as usual."

Kate refrained from commenting, but she headed for her room thinking that Edward could try a bit harder.

*

Kate came down to find the ladies gathered in the foyer in search of a distraction. She immediately recounted the latest incident involving Edward, although any response was cut short by the arrival of Oliver and Bartholomew sporting tweeds, flat caps and plus fours. Armed with rods and a bag of related paraphernalia, they were ready for a spot of fishing. Timothy Lawson, wearing a pullover and smart trousers, came along with his hands thrust into his pockets. He looked very much at a loose end.

"Has everyone got an activity arranged?" Oliver asked. "I should hate for anyone to feel at a loss."

"It's Mozart for Margaret and me," said Jane.

"And chess for Victoria and me," said Charlotte. "If anyone cares to join us, we'll be in the blue drawing room."

"Not me," said Florence. "I think a little nap in my room is in order."

"I have some magazines," said Kate. "I'll be in the living room if anyone finds themselves in need of company."

"I might try a spot of billiards," said Timothy. "I'll get Sir Charles involved. Keep him out of trouble. Actually, has anyone seen him?"

"No," said Florence. "He seems to have vanished."

Nine

Kate nodded. Yes, she would love a piece of cake. The heat of the kitchen… it was so warm as Cook cut a thick slice from a chocolate log the size of a mature oak trunk…

"Auntie?"

"Two slices, please," said Kate, stirring as Cook evaporated and the warm oven transformed into the living room fireplace – in front of which, she must have dozed off. This was the price for reading a dull article on arable farming, she surmised.

"Too warm for you?" Jane enquired.

"Yes," said Kate, closing the magazine and placing it on the seat beside her. "Aren't you practicing with Margaret?"

"Twenty minutes was enough. I really don't have the talent. She's very dedicated though. I left her rehearsing for tonight."

"Yes, I can hear her…"

Kate didn't know the tune, but it sounded delightful.

"We should take a short stroll," said Jane. "It'll wake us both up. What do you say?"

Kate's mind said no, but it was an undeniably sensible idea.

"Yes, of course. I was just about to suggest it myself."

*

Kate and Jane were well wrapped up and strolling through the grounds once more. It was good to be outside on a crisp, sunny December afternoon.

"I have to say, Jane, it's been lovely to spend some time with you. What a fine young woman you've become."

"I'm blushing, Aunt, but it's the same for me. We must stay in touch."

"Absolutely. Ties are far too easily broken."

"So… what about Christmas?" Jane asked. "Might you stay on here?"

"The atmosphere's too frosty for me. Perhaps if Edward left for New York…"

"I doubt he'll be going soon, Aunt."

"No, I suppose not. Speaking of plans… what do you have up your sleeve for next year?"

It wasn't lost on Kate that Jane's broken engagement would have left a wedding-sized gap.

"More research," said Jane, "and when the weather's good, more digs – most likely in Sussex and Kent."

"I find archaeology fascinating," said Kate. "Some of the finds are simply wonderful."

"Then you should come along to a dig."

"Oh no, I don't have the patience for it, or the eyesight, or the knees."

Just then, they spotted Bartholomew Grantley returning alone from fishing.

"That didn't last," said Kate as he headed for the house.

*

Ten minutes later, on their return, they spotted the postman heading for the side door on his bicycle.

"Good afternoon, postie," Kate called.

"Good afternoon, madam. Just the one letter for Edward. That's to say, his lordship."

Kate's initial thought was to leave it for Pritchard. However, as much as she preferred to stay out of any dealings with Edward, her concerns were for those he was currently upsetting.

"I'll take it."

The postman pulled up and handed it over.

"Much obliged, madam."

"I won't be long, Jane…"

As she headed for the house, Pritchard appeared at the side door looking somewhat perplexed.

"Shall I relieve you of that, Mrs Forbes?"

"No, thank you."

Despite Pritchard's raised eyebrows, Kate went in through the boot room, scraped her shoes on the matting, and made her way down the hallway to the library. There, she found Cook backing out looking somewhat shocked.

"Oh, he hasn't upset you too, has he?" asked Kate, already feeling annoyed. She wasn't in the habit of taxing her blood pressure these days, but this was an exception.

She went inside, where Edward was in a wingback chair half-turned away from her. It was time for a few home truths with no fluff.

Wondering where to start, she picked up a paper knife from the side table to hand to him along with the letter.

"Edward, might we talk about duty… and tradition… and how you might start pulling yourself together?"

She picked up the whiskey bottle too. He didn't need any more of that. But…

Something was wrong.

He was slumped against the wing of the chair. And, yes, now that she was looking closely, a large ceremonial dagger had been plunged deep into his side.

It took a moment for Kate's brain to configure what it all meant. And then the full seriousness of the situation struck her, forcing her back with a hop and a yelp. Unhelpfully, her backside struck something – a large vase on a plinth, which hit the floor with a terrific crash.

Her grandmother's phrase sprang instantly to mind. 'Loud enough to wake the dead', although perhaps that didn't apply on this occasion.

A moment later, Charlotte Linton came in. Almost immediately, her eyes widened.

"What have you done?" she railed.

"Are you referring to the vase or…?"

Charlotte turned and ran outside shouting, "Edward's dead, Edward's dead!" – which Kate felt added unnecessary drama to the situation. This concern was quickly borne out by the arrival of Victoria Eustace.

Kate could only wonder why she was staring, but then supposed having a knife in one hand and a bottle of whisky in the other painted a disadvantageous picture.

"I can explain," she said, although no clarification would come through for her to make use of.

Next came Timothy Lawson, no doubt from the billiards room.

"Oh my! She's lost her marbles and stabbed him!" he cried, which, for Kate, just went to show the value of thinking before speaking.

"Nonsense!" said a new voice. It was Jane, clearly working hard to control her shock. "Aunt Kate wouldn't harm a fly."

"Thank you, Jane. There's never a wrong time for the voice of reason to put in an appearance."

Acting swiftly, Jane relieved her aunt of the paper-knife and alcohol, although Kate did consider knocking back a quick glug.

Jane then turned to the body with the dagger in its side.

For Kate, this was proof of her innocence. Feeling more in touch with her faculties, she faced Timothy and the others.

"I may be a Forbes by marriage, but I'm a Bassett by birth. We attack from the front!"

Timothy's brow shot up.

"Absolutely. My apologies. For a moment it looked like…"

Now Jane addressed them.

"That dagger. Where did it come from?"

"One's missing from the rack," said Timothy.

Along from a gun cabinet, there was a display of half a dozen ceremonial daggers – with a gap in the middle.

"It seems someone held enough of a grudge against Lord Linton to take advantage of his inebriated state," said Jane.

"Who?" said Timothy.

But before she could consider it, Pritchard arrived.

"Ah," he said, spying the body. "I'll call the police."

"Yes," said Jane, "and call the doctor too, although advise him there's no hurry."

"Oh, he'll need to hurry," said Pritchard. "Cook's just collapsed."

Ten

A degree of confusion continued to reign in Kate's mind. Yes, Edward had been disliked, but what sort of maniac among them had despised him enough to kill him?

It was a thought that stayed with her beyond the arrival of Sergeant Thompson and Dr Renfrew, who were soon examining the body while Constable Hughes watched over those gathered in the living room.

Here, Kate stood by the French windows, staring out over the garden, oblivious to the murmurs of speculation bubbling up around her. Jane and Florence played no part in that though. They were at her side, quietly reassuring her that the police would soon get to the bottom of it.

Kate barely registered a response. It wasn't just the shock or a regret that she should have stayed out of it. Her thoughts were also for poor Oliver and Charlotte. They lost their brother Alistair in 1919 to Spanish flu, their mother three years ago to a stroke, their father yesterday to heart trouble, and now their brother Edward to murder. If ever those two needed to cling to the family motto, now was the time.

That said, Charlotte was sitting quietly, being comforted by Victoria and Margaret, while Oliver, having been summoned from fishing, was standing by the fireplace looking pensive.

Just then, Sergeant Thompson entered and emitted a sigh – perhaps suggesting he'd been hoping for a quiet run up to Christmas.

"Right," he announced to gain everyone's attention – although he undoubtedly already had it. "Scotland Yard have been notified and they're sending Inspector Ridley. In the meantime, let's see if we can help him."

"Good idea," said Florence. "I think we can rule Kate and Cook out of any murder investigation."

Sergeant Thompson twitched like a squirrel protecting a nut.

"With respect, madam, I'm not ruling anybody out."

"Their innocence is as plain as the nose on your face."

"Nobody's innocence is plain until the facts say so."

"You're right, of course," said Jane, attempting to smooth things over.

Thompson huffed. "Now, I'm no detective, but it's plain enough that someone here done him in. If I can lay my hands on the right chap…" he looked at Kate… "or lady, we might save Scotland Yard a bit of work. Who discovered the body?"

Kate was still a little shaken, and perhaps not thinking too clearly. But here was a question she could answer.

"That would be Cook and myself, sergeant."

"I see. I'll talk to you in a minute, Mrs…?"

"Kate Forbes."

"Yes… right… I'd also like to know the last person to see Lord Linton alive."

"That would possibly be myself," said Pritchard. "I took his lordship's coffee to him at half-past two. He was snoring."

"I assume you attempted to wake him?"

"It never occurred to me, sergeant. His lordship's moods were best avoided."

"Hmm. Did anyone else see him alive after that?"

There was no response, so Thompson returned to Pritchard.

"Unless we can find someone who saw him alive after you, you'll be viewed as a vital witness and most likely a suspect. Where's the cook?"

"In the morning room with the footman and the maid."

"Good. You and me can have a little chat once I'm finished with Mrs Forbes and the cook."

"I heard a crash," said Charlotte. "If that helps?"

"We both heard it," said Victoria.

"We went to investigate and found Mrs Forbes in the library," said Charlotte. "Sorry, Mrs Forbes, no offence."

Kate's eyes widened. "As long as they don't hang me for murder, no offence will be taken."

"Right," said Thompson, "I need to ask a blunt question. Did Lord Linton have any enemies?"

This was met with silence, causing the sergeant to raise an eyebrow.

"Interesting…"

"Edward and I were friends," said Bartholomew, pressing his half-smoked cigarette into an ashtray. "Everyone knows that."

He looked around the room for confirmation but received none.

"Also, I was nowhere near the scene," he added, a trace of anxiety affecting his voice.

"You returned early from fishing," Jane pointed out. "Aunt Kate and I saw you."

"He returned early?" said Victoria. "But… that's highly suspicious."

"Ah… yes… well… I came back before Oliver," said Bartholomew, by now more than a little flustered. "It was too cold by the river. I went up to my room for a change of clothes and stayed there for an hour reading Hemingway."

Again, his words met with no supportive noises although this time the silence seemed to crowd in on him.

"One of us is a killer," he said, "but I give you my word, on my family's honour, it wasn't me."

"No one's accusing you of murder," said Sergeant Thompson.

"No," said Jane. "We're all in a state of shock, that's all."

"That's all very well," said Timothy Lawson, "but the truth will emerge soon enough. Family honour or not. Why didn't you read by the fire in the living room?"

"What? And have the likes of you mock me for fleeing the cold? No, I stayed in my room and that's the truth."

Thompson puffed out his cheeks.

"I can see I was wrong about saving Scotland Yard a bit of work. Right, no one is to leave until Inspector Ridley says so. He shouldn't be too long in getting here. Er… I assume no one's left?"

"We're missing Sir Charles," said Florence.

"Who?" said Thompson.

"Sir Charles Sutton. He was a close friend of Lord Linton. Not this one, the previous one who died yesterday."

"Right, well, it looks like I'll have to organize a manhunt. What does he look like?"

"Just like the chap in the doorway," said Timothy.

All turned to see a rosy-cheeked Sir Charles looking slightly worse for wear.

"Are you drunk, Charles?" said Florence.

"Certainly not! Although I did pop into the Red Lion for lunch."

"The Red Lion?" queried Sergeant Thompson as if leaving the house were a crime in itself.

"Yes," said Sir Charles, "the game pie was awfully good."

The exasperated Thompson shook his head.

"Make a note of that, constable."

The constable seemed confused.

"The pie or…?"

"That Sir Charles Sutton was in the pub!"

"Yes, sarge…"

Thompson wasn't at all happy.

"I was about to have men scour the entire area."

"What for? I was in the pub," said Sir Charles. "Besides, what's all this about?"

Florence intervened.

"The police are here because Edward's been murdered."

Sir Charles seemed genuinely shocked.

"Edward…? Murdered…? Are you sure?"

"Yes, quite sure."

"Murdered… are you *sure* you're sure?"

"Yes!"

"Well… it's um… look, I really must pop upstairs for a nap. I can barely keep the old peepers open."

"Just wait there, Sir Charles," said Thompson. "I'll need a statement."

"A statement? About what?"

Yet again, the sergeant shook his head.

"Righto everyone, this is the situation. When Inspector Ridley gets here, I'm going to hand over a full set of statements. You'll all explain where you were, what you were doing, and anything pertinent you may have seen or heard."

Just then, the cook came in – her eyes red and puffy from crying. She addressed the butler.

"Sorry, Mr Pritchard, but I couldn't sit in the morning room any longer."

She then faced the sergeant.

"I never killed his lordship," she said.

"That's yet to be established," said Thompson.

"I only went to speak with him."

"You'll have plenty of time to say what happened. Just go back to the morning room and wait there."

A bleary-eyed Sir Charles snorted.

"I trust she'll be allowed back to the kitchen in time to prepare dinner?"

Thompson ignored him, instead turning to Pritchard.

"Before I speak with the staff, I want a word in private with Mrs Forbes. Is there somewhere suitable?"

"The red drawing room. This way."

Sergeant Thompson signalled to Kate.

"If you'd be so kind…" He then muttered, "I dunno – the hours I put into this job."

Kate huffed as she followed him.

"There's been a murder, sergeant. I hardly think the hours you put in are relevant. Catching the killer, that's the thing."

Thompson sighed.

"Yes, madam, but that's starting to look a lot less straightforward than I was hoping for."

Eleven

Kate and Sergeant Thompson followed Pritchard across the hallway to the threshold of another room.

"Here we are," he announced.

Thompson grunted and went inside.

Kate followed, perhaps with a little more clarity returning to her thinking.

"Do take a seat," they said at the same time.

Thompson snorted.

"I prefer to stand," he said, going to warm himself by the fire, "but feel free to—"

Kate's posterior struck the cushion before he could finish.

"Right, so," said Thompson, "before the constable takes your statement, could you explain your relationship to his lordship? By that, I mean the one in the library."

"Ah, Edward. Yes, he's the son of... that's to say he *was* the son of Lord George Linton who sadly passed away yesterday morning. I'm here as chaperone to Lady Jane Scott, daughter of the Earl of Oxley. George wanted Jane and Edward to be introduced, you see. Well, he was an eligible bachelor wasting his life away and... I don't mind saying I was having doubts."

"Let's leave all the personal entanglements to Inspector Ridley, shall we? Let's instead see if we can ascertain how you came to be in the library? Did you go there with any ill-intent?"

"What? No, I just wanted to make Edward come to his senses. He'd been rude and unpleasant, you see."

"Mrs Forbes, did you kill him?"

The question almost took Kate's breath away.

"I beg your pardon?"

"Kill him, murder him, do him in."

"Of course not."

"You're quite sure?"

"Very sure, sergeant."

"Have you any idea who did then?"

Kate waited a moment for her thumping heart to calm a little.

"Sorry, no."

"Right... and did you touch anything while you were in there?"

"No, nothing. Apart from the whisky bottle and paper knife. Oh, and I accidentally knocked over a vase."

"Yes… right. Now, you said earlier you and the cook found the body."

"She was leaving the library as I entered."

"So, the cook saw his lordship first."

"Yes."

"And then she left as you arrived. Did that leave you and the deceased alone in the room?"

"Yes."

"And did anyone else enter the library?"

"There were one or two others there soon after. I'm not sure who. I don't think my mind has quite settled. It's very confusing."

"That's quite understandable, Mrs Forbes. Now, I'd like you to remain here. The constable will be with you shortly to take a statement."

*

Twenty minutes later, having given a statement, Kate went outside with her niece for some air.

"It's so strange, Jane. In my statement, I recounted everything that happened, but… it's as if it happened to someone else. I don't mind telling you I feel a little shaky."

"It's the shock, Aunt. Be aware though, the detective from Scotland Yard won't hesitate to pick it all apart again."

"How discouraging."

"Let's prepare you, shall we?"

"I'd rather not."

"Right, understood. He'll be here soon though."

Kate sighed.

"What did you have in mind?"

"Sometimes, when we're faced with a big event, it's tempting to describe the whole thing. On an archaeological dig, I've learned to start by concentrating on the few specific details available. Cast your mind back to the moment you entered the library. What did you see?"

"Yes, well… Edward was seated in a wingback chair, leaning to one side. It's probably fair to say he'd fallen into a drunken sleep. It wouldn't have been difficult to… oh, what a thought."

"Think about what else you saw."

Kate studied the pink, white and blue heathers planted in the nearest square of the formal garden.

"I had that letter for him, so I picked up the paperknife."

"Yes, and what else?"

"The whisky bottle, half empty. There was a glass with a little of the drink still in it. And a cup of coffee. I snatched the whisky bottle away thinking I might be helping him."

"Anything else?"

"Yes… there was a handkerchief on the floor. Edward was wearing a blazer. It must have come from his breast pocket. Who's done this, Jane?"

Jane patted her aunt's arm.

"The police won't rest until they find out."

"But why kill him?"

"We can't know that yet. Time will tell though, I'm sure."

"Jane, do you think it was Cook?"

"I don't know. It's strange that she went to see Edward in the library though."

Kate shook her head.

"A violent attack by Cook seems so unlikely. Although, she's no doubt handy with a knife. No, it can't be. It had to be someone else."

"Yes, I think you're probably right."

"Then who among us has the capacity to take a life?"

"Mr Lawson and Mr Grantley came through the War."

"That's true… and I suppose we should never underestimate what we women might do given the right circumstances. To think Henry passed sentence on such cases."

Jane smiled sadly. "You must miss him."

"Every day. I can see it now. Me serving up a hearty casserole; Henry revealing the details of a ruthless poisoner. Nowadays, I usually have a crossword puzzle for company."

"He was always fun when I stayed with you."

"He thought the world of you, Jane."

"He thought the world of you, too. He used to say your logic was a bit skew-whiffy, but you were a magnificent force of Nature."

"Well, that's all changed now. Oh, perhaps not the skew-whiffy part…"

"Let's stroll a little longer, shall we?" Jane suggested.

"Yes, I think that's a good idea."

*

A short while later, feeling refreshed, Kate and Jane joined Florence, Charlotte, Margaret and Victoria in the living room. Here, some Vaughan Williams was coming from the radio speaker, perhaps helping to steer minds away from unpleasant thoughts.

"What do you think?" Florence asked them in a low, conspiratorial voice.

"About what?" Kate asked.

"About who's responsible."

"Well, we've decided it might have been a man or a woman."

"Kate, dear, that narrows it down to everyone."

"I'm just making the point that no one should think it had to be a man. That's all."

"Yes, well, I suppose you're right. But where was each of us? Can anyone say they have a witness to their innocence?"

"An alibi, you mean?"

"Yes, an alibi."

"Well, I was walking with Jane, which she can confirm…"

"I can," said Jane.

"And Victoria was with Charlotte," Kate continued. "I'm sure that's right."

Victoria nodded. "We played a little chess and did some knitting. Charlotte started on a new cardigan. It's going to be lovely."

"Oh, she's a marvel," said Florence. "So quick with the needles."

"Yes," said Charlotte, "although I never got through as much as I would normally…" but she trailed off into a tearful recollection.

"You poor thing," said Kate. "You know, detective work is hard. There are rarely footprints leading back to the culprit. Although Henry once did convict a burglar who trod in wet cement."

"The police had a shoe print…?" Florence presumed.

"Well, no, but they had a tip-off from a member of the public. When they went to the man's house, his shoes were spotlessly clean."

"Right, so how did they get him?"

"His socks had turned to concrete."

Florence pondered this for a moment before moving on.

"So where was Mr Grantley? He returned early from fishing. Do we believe he was reading Hemingway in his room the whole time?"

"We must be careful about leaping to conclusions," said Kate.

"I'm just saying he had time to act."

"Possibly, yes."

"Then there's Mr Lawson. Does he have an alibi?"

Sergeant Thompson appeared at the doorway, although Kate suspected he'd been earwigging for some time.

"Ladies, if I could ask you to save all this speculation for Inspector Ridley. Thank you."

But this wasn't the end of it. From behind him, coming along the hallway, Bartholomew Grantley could be heard.

"But you have no alibi."

"I was playing billiards," Timothy Lawson insisted.

"Did anyone see you in the billiards room?"

"No, but…"

They had now reached the doorway, where Sergeant Thompson intervened.

"If we could just keep it civil, please."

Bartholomew shrugged.

"I was just saying how Mr Lawson was playing billiards alone and that it's only a few feet from there to the library."

"Why are you pointing the finger at me?" Timothy protested. "Is it to deflect attention from yourself?"

"I'm not pointing a finger, Lawson. I'm merely stating that the billiards room is near the library, that's all."

"So is the music room, but no one's suggesting Miss Tavistock rushed off and killed Edward between sonatas."

"Now, now, gentlemen," said Thompson, heaving a sigh. "Let's leave all this to Scotland Yard."

But Timothy was undeterred.

"Be careful what you say, Barty. Nobody can vouch for you."

"I'm hardly likely to kill him."

"That's not a defence any jury will be persuaded by."

"Don't be ridiculous. Anyone who knows me knows I'd never harm anyone."

Timothy waved a hand dismissively.

"Well, somebody killed him. Oliver doesn't have an alibi and neither does the cook or the butler. And was Sir Charles really in the Red Lion?"

"None of us knows," said Kate. "I suggest we leave it for now and use the time to calm down."

"Then there's Lady Jane," said Bartholomew. "What do we really know about her?"

"I know plenty," said Kate. "You can leave my niece out of this or you'll have me to answer to."

"Alright, that's enough," said Sergeant Thompson. "Inspector Ridley should be here soon. Why don't you all find somewhere to sit quietly until he arrives."

Before anyone could respond, he marched off along the hallway muttering, "This is like herding sheep."

Twelve

Early evening saw activity in the foyer with the arrival of Inspector Leonard Ridley. From the red drawing room, Kate had heard Croft the footman summoning Sergeant Thompson and Constable Hughes. Fearing she might be a suspect, she slipped into the hallway and along to the door to the foyer.

From her vantage point, she watched Pritchard taking the inspector's hat and coat while Oliver Linton greeted him.

Poor Oliver, she thought. He'd just spent an age on the telephone explaining to various family members and friends that their presence at his father's service tomorrow would be too great a burden to bear under the circumstances.

Ridley himself, grey-haired and possibly in his early forties, stood tall in an unremarkable dark blue suit. He looked tired and irritable – no doubt less than pleased to be miles from home late in the day. Kate just hoped he had the experience needed to get to the bottom of it all sooner rather than later.

"Can I get you anything?" Oliver asked. "Tea, coffee, brandy?"

"No, I just want to take a look at the crime scene then have a word with everyone who's staying here," said Ridley in a confident voice that had perhaps left behind a working-class background. "If that's alright?"

"Yes, of course, inspector. Pritchard, could you invite everyone to gather in the living room."

"Yes, sir, right away," said Pritchard before heading towards Kate.

She took a step back into the living room as he passed on his way to round up anyone loitering in the blue drawing room, music room or billiards room.

"Has the photographer been?" Ridley asked Thompson as they came unhurriedly by.

"About half an hour ago, sir."

"And what about fingerprints."

"It's all in hand. We've also searched the deceased's rooms. Nothing there though."

"Good, I'll take a look myself a bit later."

"Once you're done with the crime scene, we're ready to take the body away. Oh, and all the statements are waiting for you."

"Well done, sergeant," said Ridley as they disappeared into the library. "I do like to see efficiency…"

Kate wondered. What did she make of Ridley of the Yard? She supposed, most of all, she was impressed by his stride – measured and deliberate, as if haste might mean him missing something.

*

Despite the Christmas tree and festive decorations, the mood in the living room was understandably sombre. It was a tone further affected by the presence of Inspector Ridley who was facing those gathered within from one side of the fireplace.

"As you're no doubt aware, I'm here to investigate the murder of Lord Edward Linton."

"May he rest in peace," said Florence.

"Indeed. Now, this event took place sometime between Mr Pritchard taking coffee to the library at half-past two and the discovery of the body at ten-to-three. If anyone has any information not in their statement, now's a good time to rectify it. I'll be speaking to each of you soon enough and I'd like to go to bed tonight knowing that nothing has been omitted by anyone."

"Perhaps I can help you there, inspector," said Kate, wanting badly to aid the cause of justice. "I've weighed up some of the factors that have been swirling around in my head. I might be able to filter out some of the more extraneous aspects for you."

"Sorry, who exactly are you, madam?"

Florence cut in.

"May I introduce Mrs Katherine Forbes, widow of the late judge, Henry Forbes CBE and sister of the late Annette Scott, Countess of Oxley. She was also at school with two of the Brook-Castletons and is a third cousin twice removed from the Duke of Rutland."

"The pub in Mayfair?" queried Sir Charles. "I've been twice removed from there too!"

Ridley waved them away.

"I haven't got time for all this. Who can talk to me about Lord Linton?"

"Which one?" asked Sir Charles.

"Edward. How was he?"

Sir Charles frowned.

"Before or after his death?"

Ridley took a breath, but before he could speak, Florence cut in.

"You'll have to excuse Sir Charles's terrible sense of humour," she said, apologetically.

"Edward was pleased with himself," said Timothy Lawson, taking a cigarette from a silver case.

"Yes, well, someone else clearly wasn't quite so pleased," said Ridley.

"My brother was a troubled man," said Oliver.

"Is that so?" said Ridley, raising an eyebrow. "A little birdy told the sergeant that you and your brother were arguing quite a bit. Would you care to explain?"

"It was nothing," said Oliver.

"Oh really?"

Timothy lit his cigarette and emitted a steady stream of smoke.

"Oliver and Edward failed to see eye-to-eye on how the Linton estate might best be managed," he said.

But Ridley's gaze remained on Oliver.

"You were an equal in making those decisions, were you?"

"No," said Oliver, "after our father's death, my brother had the final say on all such matters."

"Are we saying you didn't approve of his ideas?"

"Something like that, yes."

"And am I right in thinking your brother had no offspring, meaning the title now falls to you."

Oliver paused before answering.

"Yes."

If the room had been silent beforehand, that silence somehow deepened and intensified.

"Inspector Ridley, I never killed my brother. I wouldn't... and even if I'd wanted to... well, you all know I was fishing at the river. I had to be summoned."

"Don't worry," said Ridley, "I'll be looking into your fishing session as soon as I can."

"Excuse me, inspector," said a flustered Florence. "You're not seriously making Oliver a suspect?"

"Everyone's a suspect until I can rule them out, madam. Constable, let me have the statements. I want to go over them as soon as I can."

Oliver sighed.

"Look, why don't you set up shop in the study. Pritchard will show you the way."

"Thanks, that's very much appreciated."

"Will you be taking dinner with us, inspector?" asked Sir Charles. "It's sausages."

"No, there's a killer in our midst and I intend to find out who it is. Obviously, if someone could send some sausages to the study, that would be helpful."

Thirteen

Once again, everyone sat down to dinner with an absence at the head of the table. Of course, this time there would be no late arrival by Lord Edward Linton.

As a mark of respect, the men wore dark jackets and ties, while muted hues also dominated the women's choices, from Jane's midnight blue silk woven fabric dress to Charlotte's shapeless long grey jumper.

As they began the soup course, the day's events weighed heavily upon proceedings, especially for Oliver and Charlotte, the surviving Lintons. Understandably, for everyone, conversation was proving difficult.

"Another sunny day and frosty night," said Kate, in the wake of a lengthy hiatus.

"Yes," said Jane. "Lots of stars out tonight."

This was followed by more silence.

"Excellent soup," Jane eventually added.

"Mmm, winter broth, just the thing," said Kate.

"One of us is a killer," said Florence.

This sparked a much longer silence in which the occasional slurp of soup felt like an intrusion.

It was Sir Charles who eventually broke it.

"Ridley looks young. I wonder if he's any good at his job."

"I'm sure he is," said Kate.

"He looks inexperienced to me," said Sir Charles.

"He must be at least forty," Bartholomew Grantley insisted.

"That's what I said," Sir Charles countered. "Young!"

"It couldn't be any worse," said Timothy Lawson.

"It could," said Sir Charles. "Had they arrested Cook, Pritchard would've made our dinner."

"That's in very poor taste," said Florence.

"As would our meal be," said Sir Charles. "Of course, if Cook's the murderer, she could strike again, tonight, armed with a knife while we're in our beds. Or she could use a different method… such as poison."

Florence, slurping a spoonful of soup, let out a messy splutter.

Indeed, everyone peered into their bowls, including Kate, who was beginning to wish she had stayed at home in Sandham-on-Sea. Sir Charles, however, simply laughed and took another spoonful.

"We don't have to stay," said Bartholomew. "Unless the police press charges, we're free to go."

"Now wouldn't that make a pretty picture," said Timothy Lawson. "Mr Bartholomew Grantley is all too keen to flee the scene of a murder. I wonder what Scotland Yard would make of that?"

"Leaving Linton Hall doesn't make one a suspect," Bartholomew insisted.

"Make sure you wish us all a Happy Christmas before you leave," said Timothy. "And don't fret about Lord George Linton's service. No doubt, you'll be there in spirit representing your splendid family."

Bartholomew huffed but said nothing more.

"It's incredible to be in the midst of a murder investigation," said Florence. "What do you make of it all, Kate?"

Kate shook her head.

"I wouldn't know. My experience is, to say the least, limited."

"Nonsense. All those countless evenings Henry explained cases to you over dinner? I for one think that counts as extensive experience."

"Ah yes," said Timothy. "Your late husband was a judge. I understand he was quite a figure on the circuit."

"He was."

"They say you make a lot of enemies."

"Yes, indeed. The criminal world…"

"I was referring to the other judges."

"Ah."

"But as you say, you have no experience yourself."

"No," Kate conceded, "but what one lacks in experience, one can make up for by 'having a go'. I'm no detective, but perhaps I was wrong to say I've no idea as to what happened."

Timothy raised an eyebrow.

"Would you care to elaborate?"

"Not at this time, no."

"Could we talk about something else while we eat?" Bartholomew requested.

"Hear, hear to that," said Oliver.

"Yes," said Florence. "Perhaps Lady Jane might talk a little more about her interest in archaeology. She's been on many local digs, haven't you, dear."

"I've been on a few, yes."

Sir Charles nodded.

"They say an archaeologist can discern an entire story from the smallest of clues."

"It's true," said Jane. "A team working under Professor Peregrine Nash discovered the site of a Roman villa from a single piece of mosaic discovered in a field. As part of the effort, I went up in a hot air balloon during a drought and saw the outline. They uncovered an almost complete mosaic floor."

"Marvellous," said Margaret. "What are you currently working on?"

"Nothing right now, but as you know, historical research is my thing, so hopefully there'll soon be more of that. I'll also get along to some digs next year."

"Is history a career for a woman?" Timothy asked.

"It's difficult but not impossible," said Jane. "I've worked on a few research projects. One of them had me going over dusty old manuscripts for five months."

"So, it's just a hobby until you marry?" Sir Charles wondered.

"Well…"

"I'm sure Lady Jane will soon find the right man," said Victoria Eustace. "Then all her problems will melt away."

"Problems?" said Jane. "What problems?"

Victoria declined to say.

"I knew an old chap," Timothy mused. "Winstanley, his name was. Lived in our village. He was a Professor of Medieval History. Bumbling old fool, if you ask me."

"Well, it's unlikely for me," said Jane, "but I'd love to hold that kind of post."

"Professor Lady Jane Scott?"

But Timothy laughed it off no sooner he'd said it.

For Kate, this rankled. Why should Jane have to explain herself to someone like Timothy Lawson?

"How will Inspector Ridley know he's got the right person?" Margaret Tavistock asked. "I mean, what if they won't admit to it?"

"They use a logical process," said Timothy. "They make a list of all those who had a motive, then they narrow it down by omitting those who lacked the opportunity to commit the crime. There's a further trimming down of the number by looking at who had access to the method of murder. What they call the means. Why not try it."

"Try what?"

"Being the detective."

Margaret frowned.

"How would I do that?"

"You simply pick someone and name a motive."

Margaret flushed slightly.

"I wouldn't know where to start."

"I've already told you. Pick someone. Or if you like, I'll pick someone for you. Oliver, perhaps."

"That's most unfair," said Florence.

"Unfair suggests subjectivity, but the detective process is quite objective. Now Oliver won't mind, I'm sure. Will you?"

Oliver declined to comment, preferring instead to finish his soup in silence.

"Does this really name the killer?" asked Margaret, worriedly looking into various faces around the table.

"No," said Jane. "Without evidence or a confession, the methodology described simply allows the detective to consider ruling out anyone who fails one of the tests."

"I like it," said Sir Charles. "It tells us who to avoid bumping into in the middle of the night."

"Right," said Timothy, undeterred. "Means? That's easy. The dagger was in the library."

"Surely, this is too grisly for the dinner table, Lawson," said Bartholomew. "Even for you."

"Hey, you were quite happy to offer me up to the police. If found guilty, I'd hang. This is far less grisly than that. Besides, we might get to the bottom of it."

"Pah," Bartholomew huffed.

But Timothy Lawson seemed determined to see it through.

"Right, so Oliver had access to the means, but did he have a motive? Well, I'd say plenty of people down the years have killed for land and money. So, what about the opportunity to commit the crime?"

"Oliver was fishing," said Charlotte.

"Yes, but delicate Barty came back early because it was too chilly for his poor constitution. That gave Oliver a chance to come back soon after, do the deed, and then hurry back to the river where he'd be found later by a distressed footman."

"It's a fanciful tale," said Florence. "I, for one, find it quite unpleasant."

"It's the method Ridley will be using," Timothy pointed out.

"Good grief, Lawson," said Oliver, finally reacting. "My brother is dead. Let's show some respect."

But Sir Charles gazed upon Oliver and sighed.

"The police will think it's you, dear boy. Oliver Linton, the ninth Baron Linton, of Woodvale in the County of Sussex. You disliked your brother and felt you were the right calibre of heir to restore dignity to the family. You called him a disgrace and now you'll gain through inheritance because Edward had no offspring."

Oliver waved it away.

"I'm sure nobody here suspects me of being a murderer. And I'm equally sure Inspector Ridley will come to the same conclusion. Now, let that be an end to it over dinner."

Sir Charles nodded.

"As you wish, *Lord Linton.*"

Fourteen

After dinner, extra chairs were brought into the music room where everyone had gathered to hear Margaret play Mozart on a beautiful rosewood baby grand piano. Her original selection of bright, fizzing pieces had of course been replaced by more reflective choices to fit the mood.

Indeed, it was an atmosphere further enhanced by candlelight, a roaring fire, and cigarette smoke spiralling lazily upward from several sources.

Kate found the music divine. What with a glass of sherry before dinner, a glass of claret with her meal, and now a glass of port during a quiet adagio, she felt as if she were floating away on a soft fluffy…

"Right!" said Inspector Ridley, his sudden entry causing Kate to jump awake and Margaret to stop playing.

"Ah, Ridley," said Sir Charles Sutton. "How were the sausages?"

"Never mind that. I've just finished going over the statements and I'm not happy."

Before continuing, he reached for the light switch to illuminate the scene more effectively.

"It seems everyone here is innocent, saw nothing suspicious, and feels they've contributed to the utmost with the police. Well, I'm going to help you all do a little better. I'll be interviewing the staff first thing in the morning, then I'd be obliged if you'd all make yourselves available after breakfast. I intend to get to the bottom of this and some of you may have information that can help me."

"So," Sir Charles ventured, "you haven't a clue."

Ridley disregarded him.

"I'd urge each of you as you rest overnight to think hard. Did you see anything, no matter how seemingly insignificant, that struck you as odd." He checked his watch. "Right, it's half-past nine. I'm just going to have a quick word with the cook, then I've arranged for a room at the Red Lion pub. I'll see you all back here in the morning."

"You could spend the night at Linton Hall, inspector," said Florence.

Sir Charles baulked.

"With a murderer on the loose? He'd be mad to stay here."

"Just one other thing," said Ridley. "I trust nobody's thinking of leaving. I'd take a very dim view if anyone did."

"Did you hear that, Barty?" said Timothy.

Bartholomew ignored him.

"Right," said Ridley, "I'll leave a constable here should anyone wish to report anything."

"I'll take that as you wishing to keep an eye on us," said Sir Charles.

Just then, a constable arrived with the cook.

"Ah, Mrs Parker," said Ridley. "If you'd like to step into the study."

"Poor Cook," said Florence, watching them go. "I wonder what he's going to ask her."

Sir Charles almost gagged.

"Well, he's hardly likely to ask if she's got any more sausages!"

*

An hour or so later, Kate and Jane were making their way upstairs.

"What a strange day," said Kate. "I'm completely worn out."

Jane nodded sympathetically.

"According to Inspector Ridley, we're to spend our time between now and the morning thinking of any odd happenings."

"Yes, well, I can't guarantee that won't transform into a deep sleep. Perhaps I'll give it some thought over breakfast."

At her bedroom door, Kate invited her niece inside.

"Just for a moment."

Once inside, she smiled sadly.

"Jane, I was hoping we'd have a pleasant couple of days together. Lots of catching up… sharing hopes… sharing dreams. You've been through quite a bit this past year."

"And so have you, Aunt."

"True…"

"I don't want you to worry about me. I'm fine."

Kate gave a little nod. "Very well."

"Now you get some rest and I'll see you in the morning."

"Yes, alright…"

But Kate's brow furrowed.

"There's just one thing, Jane. It's probably nothing, but… why did Cook go to see Edward?"

"Perhaps he had some views about dinner."

"It's possible, but Pritchard relays that sort of thing. I wonder if there's something else going on."

"You're not thinking of looking into it, are you?"

"Oh, it's so chilly in here. Has that window been left open a crack?" Not for the first time, Kate checked it, and even nudged the top sash, which rattled to confirm the presence of the dreaded gap. "At home, I plug draughty gaps with strips of damp newspaper, which I leave to set for the winter. They probably wouldn't like that here though."

"Aunt Kate? You were saying?"

"Oh… well, I'd be a lot happier if I knew the right person was facing justice, that's all."

"You mean you'd hate Inspector Ridley to leap to the wrong conclusion?"

"Yes, perhaps we could… weigh things up."

"I doubt Inspector Ridley encourages amateurs to involve themselves."

"We wouldn't be *involved*, Jane. We'd simply be absorbing information and trying to make sense of it."

"Isn't that what Inspector Ridley does?"

Fifteen

Shortly after breakfast, a well-wrapped Kate and Jane took advantage of the opportunity to stroll through the sunny yet crisp, chilly garden and beyond. With Ridley of the Yard wanting to see them at some point soon, it seemed wise to be fully roused.

At the Linton Estate's southern boundary, they took in a breath-taking view of the valley, with farmland out to the east and the village to the west. Here, the river meandered through low-lying land that would remain white with frost until the sun rose quite a bit higher.

"How are you bearing up?" Jane asked.

"I'm alright," said Kate. "It just feels a bit unreal, that's all."

"Yes, it does."

"I said yesterday we might take an interest in the investigation. I'm not so sure now."

"After what you've been through, it's hardly surprising. Let's talk about something else."

"Yes, let's."

"You mentioned finding archaeology interesting."

"I do, Jane. It's a fascinating subject."

"Then you must come along to a dig – *and* before you mention your knees again, you could simply pay us a visit."

"A visit?"

"Imagine it… I'd drive you to a fine inn where we'd have dinner, and you'd stay in a plump bed. Then, in the morning, we'd have a cooked breakfast and a stroll. Then we'd spend an hour at the dig site where you'd get to meet everyone and see what's what. After that it would be lunch, a snooze, some high tea, a stroll, drinks, dinner, and a good night's rest. Then I'd drive you home the following morning."

"Jane, you're right. Archaeology sounds just the thing."

"Leave it with me. I'll organise something."

"Are you sure it wouldn't be an imposition?"

"Absolutely not. Consider it an arrangement."

Kate felt a warm glow.

"Wonderful."

On their return, they came around the kitchen side of the house, where Cook was outside the back door discussing something with Gloria the maid.

"Good morning," Kate called.

"Good morning, madam," both replied, although Gloria, seemingly preoccupied with something, went back inside.

"Thank goodness yesterday's behind us," said Kate. "What an ordeal. Especially for you, Mrs Parker."

"For you too, madam. You had the same shock as I did."

"Yes, about that…"

This was a chance to question Cook, but now, face to face, it felt intrusive. Kate wasn't an investigator. She had no right. And, indeed, no desire.

And yet…

Wasn't this an ideal opportunity to get to the bottom of something that had been troubling her?

"Cook… I'm no detective, and I certainly don't wish to pry, but yesterday I went to see his lordship to hand over a letter. I was just wondering why you went to see him."

"No particular reason, madam. Just kitchen matters."

"Did he summon you?"

"No, but… well… I had to see him. It was important."

"In what way?"

"I… just needed to speak to him, that's all."

"Was it a secret?" Jane asked. "Something his lordship wanted to surprise everyone with?"

"Yes," said Cook.

"And are you able to tell us the nature of this secret?"

"It was nothing, your ladyship. A matter of beef or duck, that's all."

Kate wasn't convinced.

"Mrs Parker, this is a very serious matter. Someone will hang for murder. If you're hiding something, you must tell. If not to us, then to Inspector Ridley. It's imperative that the culprit is identified."

"Yes, madam. I'm as keen as you are to see justice done."

"Right, well, there we are then. Justice must be done. We're all agreed. We'll say good morning to you, Cook."

Kate and Jane withdrew and continued with the final stage of their walk.

"We're not investigating then?" said Jane.

"No. Well, yes. That's to say, we might be. Do you think Cook's a killer?"

"No, but she does seem to be hiding something."

"Ah, there's Pritchard," said Kate, spotting the butler by the boot room. She wondered if this might be a chance to make some progress.

"Good morning," she called.

"Good morning, madam. Not too chilly for you, I trust."

"No, we're wrapped up like a couple of Egyptian mummies. But may I ask you a question or two?"

"Of course. I'll help if I can."

"What's Cook like as a person?"

For a fraction of a second, Pritchard gave Kate a borderline insolent stare. It, of course, vanished instantly.

"I'm not sure I understand."

"I've always assumed she's utterly trustworthy."

"I'm sure she is, madam, but alas I cannot discuss the matter on police instructions."

"Really? That's frustrating to hear. It's not as if I'm investigating the case."

"They were most insistent."

"Yes, well… thank you, Pritchard."

Aunt and niece strolled on.

"I'm more certain now," said Kate. "If we care about justice, it won't hurt to keep our eyes and ears open."

They returned to the house by the front door, enjoying the warmth of the foyer as they entered.

"Morning, ladies," greeted Bartholomew Grantley. He was coming down the stairs. "Been taking the air, have we?"

"We have," said Kate as she removed her coat. "Taking the air and asking questions."

"Questions? I fear we'll have enough of those when Inspector Ridley arrives."

"No doubt," said Kate.

"Lady Jane," said Bartholomew, shifting his focus, "I must say I'm fascinated by your interest in archaeology. All that digging about must be most rewarding."

"You've hit the nail on the head there," said Jane, "but patience is everything. That probably explains my interest in historical research. I have the patience for it."

"Hmmm, dusty old parchments, you mean. No, this digging malarky sounds fun. A bunch of friends, the summer sun, all off to the pub afterwards. Yes, I can see it. I've worked out the truth of your little distraction, Lady Jane. You're a fun-seeker."

Kate stepped in.

"Yes, archaeology… it's fascinating how little details can give clues to what really happened in the past."

"Yes," said Bartholomew, "although I suspect there's also the danger of bending a few sparse details to fit a favoured theory."

With that, he took himself off into the hallway, whistling a tune.

"I dare say we can put our coats away ourselves," said Kate, opening the cloakroom door and indicating that Jane should hand her own garment over.

From inside the small space, Kate continued.

"In my opinion, there's something far more concerning than the villain getting away with it."

"You mean the wrong person being hanged for murder."

"Precisely," said Kate, emerging again. "We'll keep an eye on the progress the police make. If all's well, then we can rest. But if things go awry…"

"We should make sure we've done our bit?"

"Exactly. So, what do you think of Mr Grantley?"

"Barty? The one thing that troubles me is the way he reacted to Edward stating his intention to decamp to New York."

"Yes, he acted very oddly at that point. Certainly, the warmth he'd been showing towards Edward seemed to evaporate."

"That said, if we're to be even-handed we might balance our thinking with the fact that Barty had nothing obvious to gain from Edward's death."

"Yes," said Kate. "Oliver's the real beneficiary in all this. The thing is, I've known him since he was a boy."

"True, but there might be a hidden side to him."

"A dark side, you mean. Yes, that's always a possibility. You never can tell."

A few moments later, they joined a growing number in the living room – all waiting for Inspector Ridley's arrival. Indeed, with Oliver and Margaret visible in the garden, and Timothy Lawson outside on the terrace smoking a cigarette, only Charlotte was unaccounted for.

"Where is he?" said an impatient Sir Charles Sutton, as much for the household as the constable standing by the door.

If the constable knew, he wasn't saying.

Kate meanwhile observed Victoria watching Timothy. Perhaps she admired him. He was a darkly interesting man – the kind who, down the ages, had proven fascinating to no end of unfortunate women.

But Kate's eyes suddenly widened.

"Jane," she whispered. "It's probably nothing to do with the murder, but the night before last, I overheard an argument between Timothy and Edward. They were trying to keep their voices down, but I caught part of it as I was coming up the stairs."

"What did you hear?"

"I'm not sure exactly, but it was something to do with the War."

Sir Charles took his pipe from his pocket.

"What a bother!" he announced. "I'm sorry Edward's gone, but he was a wastrel. He liked to play at being an art collector, but nobody took him seriously. I mean, look at that monstrosity."

All eyes turned to the bold, modernist painting on the wall.

Meanwhile, Sir Charles lit his pipe, creating a billowing fog that engulfed all those nearby. In response, Kate coughed politely and took a step back, as did Jane.

"What do you think of it, Victoria?" Sir Charles asked.

"Me?"

"Yes, you."

"I'm no art expert, Sir Charles. I really wouldn't know."

"But you knew Edward in Paris. Is that the sort of thing people pay good money for over there?"

"I was only there a short time with Charlotte during the summer. As for Lord Edward Linton, I assumed he was a successful dealer, but as I say, I'm no expert."

"I doubt any of us are," said Florence, although her demeanour suggested a dislike for the painting in question.

"Oh, where *is* Ridley?" Sir Charles insisted. "Has he forgotten there's a killer on the loose?"

"I'm sure he hasn't," said Jane.

"We should've put him up here last night where we could've kept an eye on him!"

"I'm sure he was very comfortable at the pub," said Florence.

"Hmm…" said Sir Charles before puffing some more on his pipe.

The conversation continued for a further half hour before Inspector Ridley finally entered the living room.

"Sorry to have kept you waiting," he said. "I was delayed on the telephone to Scotland Yard. Developments in another case."

"Yes, they serve strong beer at the Red Lion," said Sir Charles. "I always get a hangover too."

"Serious crimes don't always come along one at a time," said Ridley, dismissing the notion. "I wish they did. But I wouldn't mind some coffee."

Pritchard nodded and made for the door.

"Oh, any chance of some buttered toast with that coffee?" Ridley added.

"Of course, sir."

"Inspector?" Kate asked. "Who will you be interviewing first?"

"Yes, good question…"

"Only, we're due at the church soon."

"Right, well, I'll be interviewing the cook again, and then you, Mrs Forbes."

"The service is at ten, inspector."

"Don't worry about that. We can talk on the way to the church."

Kate frowned. "If you insist."

"I do."

"I must say though, at my age, I don't like the idea of arriving at God's house being questioned about my role in a murder."

Sixteen

On a crisp sunny morning, several cars prepared to leave Linton Hall in convoy. Jane was behind Gertie's wheel, with Margaret alongside her. Meanwhile, a somewhat disgruntled Kate was seated in the back of a police car waiting for Inspector Ridley to get in beside her.

In some ways, it felt like a low point. Kate had always operated with a keen sense of purpose. But over the past six months, that river of energy had slowed to a trickle and her confidence had waned.

However, sitting in a police car, buffeted by the winds of fortune, she felt something. It seemed an unlikely source, but yes, the possibility of a killer getting away with it… and letting another take their place at the gallows… somehow, her own concerns paled in comparison.

In fact, for the first time in months, it seemed appropriate for something of her old, confident, forthright self to make a partial return, because… this case, this challenge… it was restoring her sense of purpose. She was Mrs Kate Forbes. That used to mean something. And it would once more. Even if it might only be temporary.

Ridley got in and pulled the door to.

"I know this isn't the way you wanted to arrive at the church, Mrs Forbes, but I still have some questions that need answering."

"That's no problem, inspector. It's a very comfortable vehicle."

"Thank you, madam," said the constable at the wheel as they pulled away. "It's a Daimler."

"A Daimler. I'd imagine it was quite expensive."

"Yes, madam, the West Sussex Constabulary bought it second-hand from an industrialist in Chichester."

"How enterprising," said Kate. "I do like to see initiative."

"Could we forget the car?" Ridley insisted. "Mrs Forbes, why did you take that letter from the postman?"

"You already know the answer. I wanted to have words with Edward. He'd been a rotten host and seemed to have no desire to fulfil his obligations. Delivering the post seemed the perfect opportunity."

"Did you feel you needed an excuse to see him?"

"Well, yes. I didn't feel I'd get far if I simply barged in. He might've taken against me. My subterfuge was designed to put him at ease. Then we'd talk."

"You don't think he'd have asked why the butler or footman hadn't brought the post?"

"I planned to tell him the staff were busy but that the letter might be important. He'd be pleased with me then, you see?"

"Was that likely?"

"That he'd be pleased with me?"

"No, that the staff would be too busy to put the master of the house first?"

"Ah, you're forgetting – Edward was drunk. He'd hardly pay attention to such details. No, I positioned myself perfectly. Only, someone got to him before me."

"Yes, and not just to have words."

"No, indeed."

Kate wondered if that was that. But what about theories? What about the next step? Of course, she was a lowly amateur and he was a high ranking professional. But surely he might value other opinions. Did it matter where they came from?

She took a breath.

"Inspector, I've given this some thought. I'd say the murderer knew Edward would be dozing. If we accept that, then we're looking for someone who…"

"Mrs Forbes! This is not a joint investigation. Your only role is to answer my questions."

"Yes, of course, but please don't forget we both serve a higher calling. The pursuit of justice."

"I assure you, madam, I haven't forgotten it. Now, where was I?"

"We were taking into account who knew Edward would be in a vulnerable state, and we were about to narrow the field by considering motives."

*

The cars came to a halt outside St Luke's Church, the Linton family's place of worship for almost 150 years. The church itself predated the Lintons' arrival by a further 150 years but, vitally, the first baron's funding restored a roof in danger of collapse. Hence his image in one of the stained-glass windows. There was also a private crypt beneath the church which held the remains of all the previous barons and their wives, while the lesser Lintons were buried in the adjoining graveyard.

Outside the church, a few villagers had gathered to pay their respects and no doubt share any available gossip. Certainly, recent events at Linton Hall had the potential to keep local jaws exercised for months.

"One more thing before you get out," said Inspector Ridley. "Let's talk about the letter. Did you have any idea of its contents?"

"No," said Kate. "I just grabbed it from the postman before Pritchard could get to it."

"Is this the letter?" he asked, taking an envelope from his pocket.

"Yes, that looks like the one."

"This is an invitation to join a golf club."

"A golf club? Oh, I'm thinking you're barking up the wrong tree there, inspector. I'd suggest the golf club has no bearing on the matter."

Ridley let out a heavy sigh.

"This idea to give Edward a good talking to… are you sure it came to you on the spur of the moment? Or might you have planned to intercept the post?"

"I beg your pardon?"

"You were consumed by frustration, perhaps?"

"You sound like the counsel for the prosecution, inspector. For the record, I wasn't consumed by anything. I simply came across the postman bringing a letter for Edward. As I've explained, it gave me the idea of using it to get myself into the library. Only now, I wish I hadn't bothered. My late husband would say we're often the architects of our own downfall."

"Mrs Forbes, please. In your statement, you say you saw no-one else on the way to the library."

Kate thought for a moment.

"That's correct."

"So you knocked on the door…?"

"No, as I said in my statement, Cook was coming out. I can see now that she was in a state of shock. I didn't see it then."

"So then you took one look at Edward and left the library to raise the alarm."

"Don't try to trip me up, inspector. As per my statement, I went there to berate him. And that's what I did."

"You berated the deceased?"

"It sounds silly when you put it like that."

"Would you describe yourself as an observant person, Mrs Forbes?"

"Very much so. You have to remember I was expecting to rouse a drunk."

"Only your task was suddenly elevated from the difficult to the impossible."

"Quite so."

"Well, I don't suppose we can hold up Lord Linton's service any longer."

"No, indeed, although this whole business has taken a toll. There should have been fifty or sixty people here today. Now we'll be lucky to make double figures."

"Alright, Mrs Forbes. We'll speak again, I'm sure."

"Yes, inspector. In the meantime, I'll let you know if I come up with any fresh insights."

She got out of the car and closed the door behind her. Was the old Kate Forbes returning? The one with the skew-whiffy logic? The magnificent force of Nature?

Perhaps.

Seventeen

Passing through the old lychgate, Kate arrived at the church door just behind Charlotte and Oliver, although she held back a little while the vicar greeted and consoled the bereaved.

"My sincere condolences," he said. "Your dear father will be long remembered for his kindness and good deeds."

"Thanks, vicar," said Oliver before leading his sister inside.

Kate stepped forward and announced herself.

"Mrs Kate Forbes. A friend of the Lintons and an occasional visitor to your lovely parish."

"Welcome, Mrs Forbes. Are you staying at the hall?"

"Yes, at least until things have settled down a little for Oliver and Charlotte."

"Yes, such tragic times for them."

"Indeed."

Inside, St Luke's was a modest establishment, with a dozen rows of pews that could seat six worshippers either side of the aisle – ample room for the small number in attendance. The wooden altar was plain, possibly quite new, but the main attraction was the large arched stained-glass window depicting St Luke the Evangelist. Facing east, it blazed with low winter sunlight.

As Oliver and Charlotte made their way to the front, Kate paused a moment to offer a little prayer for her parents, her sister, her husband, and now for George and Edward. She then looked for Jane.

"Ah, there she is…"

Her niece was seated near the front alongside Margaret and Victoria. Kate, however, changed her mind and opted to join Florence much nearer the back.

They sat for a while in silence before Florence spoke.

"What did the inspector want?"

"Lots of answers, Florrie. I told them everything I know in my statement, but Scotland Yard teach their detectives to ask further questions. I think it's designed to catch us out."

She glanced all around, including over her shoulder, where Inspector Ridley was sitting directly behind her.

He smiled. "Ladies."

Florence tutted and encouraged Kate to join her in moving seats.

Once they had relocated, Kate leaned close to her friend.

"He wondered if I might be consumed by frustration."

"I beg your pardon?"

"With Edward's behaviour. In fact, frustrated enough to act in anger. Then he made me feel a fool for not realizing right away that Edward was… no longer with us."

"That's appalling, Kate. It's not as if you come across dead bodies every day."

"No, but let's not hold it against him. Should I find myself in a position to help Scotland Yard, I'll do so."

"That's very commendable."

"It is indeed," said Sir Charles, sitting across the aisle but clearly having listened in on their conversation.

"Thank you, Sir Charles," said Kate, "but the discussion on finding the culprit is a private matter."

"Finding the culprit?" said Timothy Lawson, who was seated behind Sir Charles. "We're hardly short of suspects. Sir Charles included, on the basis of him disappearing around the time of the murder."

"I had a pub lunch!" Sir Charles insisted. "I think that's beyond dispute."

"I hardly think a bunch of drunks in the Red Lion can be reliable alibis," said Timothy.

"It's true, Sir Charles," said Bartholomew from the row behind Timothy. "You might've run back to the house, grabbed a dagger from the display rack…"

"Run? I had three pints of beer, three double whiskeys and a pie!"

Bartholomew shrugged. "Alright, *staggered* back to the house."

"What?" scoffed Timothy. "After all that I'm surprised he managed to *find* the house."

Sir Charles harrumphed. "The police checked the pub. They confirmed I was there. That means it was most likely one of you two. From what I've heard, one of you was playing billiards alone, and the other returned from fishing early."

"Welcome to St Luke's," intoned the vicar from the front.

Florence nudged Kate.

"I'm surprised they haven't arrested us all."

Kate baulked at that.

"Please don't give them ideas, Florrie."

The vicar raised his voice.

"It's with great sadness that we gather to mark the passing of a dear loved one and friend, the Right Honourable Lord George Linton, the seventh Baron Linton, of Woodvale in the county of Sussex…"

*

After the service, the congregation ambled outside into the sunshine.

"Well, here we are," said Kate, uncertain of what to say.

"It was lovely to sing Abide With Me," said Margaret. "Such a lovely hymn."

"They sang it at the Football Association Cup Final at Wembley in May," said Bartholomew. "I was there. Arsenal versus Cardiff. A terrific game."

"Margaret's right. It's a lovely hymn," said Jane, steering them away from football. "Do you have an interest in sacred music?"

"Not especially," said Margaret, "although I did enjoy Mozart's Requiem once in London."

Jane addressed Bartholomew.

"We lost a lot of music when Henry the Eighth closed the monasteries. Most people don't know the authorities burned the choir books. Frankly, we're lucky to have Tallis and Byrd."

Bartholomew raised an eyebrow.

"Are we indeed?"

As he withdrew, Margaret let slip a smile.

So did Kate.

"Speaking of music," she said, "I'm already looking forward to this proper celebration of George's life come the spring."

"Yes," said Margaret, "the whole village singing lots of hymns. I can't think of a more fitting tribute."

"Ah," said Kate, spotting a chance to get to Inspector Ridley by the church door. "Excuse me, ladies."

A moment later, she was with Ridley.

"It was a lovely service, wasn't it, inspector."

"Er, yes. Very poignant."

"I think you'd have liked the seventh Baron Linton, or plain old George as some of us knew him."

"With respect, Mrs Forbes, it's the eighth Baron Linton I'm interested in. Now, if you'll excuse me."

Ridley's focus was already fixed on Bartholomew Grantley.

"Mr Grantley, before you leave, I must ask you a couple of questions."

"Really," huffed Bartholomew. "You shouldn't listen to idle accusations echoing around a church. People get all kinds of fanciful ideas."

"Never mind that. Around the time of the murder, you were fishing with Oliver Linton. Only, you came back early."

"It was freezing down by the river and I'm not a dedicated angler."

Ridley seemed to notice something; possibly Kate listening in.

"Constable, escort Mrs Forbes away, would you?"

"Where to, sir?"

"I really don't mind."

"I'm perfectly capable of removing myself," said Kate.

Before the constable could act, she withdrew to be with Jane who was standing with Margaret beside Gertie.

"I'll take a ride with Barty and Victoria," said Margaret.

"Thank you," said Kate. "Jane, you don't mind driving while I think, do you?"

Before long they were seated comfortably in Gertie and heading back to the hall.

"Things aren't going too smoothly with the case," said Kate. "I get the feeling Inspector Ridley's fishing around in the hope of a lucky catch. And speaking of fishing, would Oliver really kill his own brother? I've always found him a good sort. I mean, we only saw glimpses of the relationship between the two of them, but… oh, I don't know."

"Some families argue," said Jane. "It doesn't make them killers."

"Too true," said Kate. "Otherwise, half of England would be bumped off over Christmas."

Jane smiled.

"As you know, Inspector Ridley concentrates on motive. Oliver stood to gain."

"Yes, well, I can see that doesn't help him."

"He also has no alibi for the time of the murder."

"Yes, but apart from all that, don't you think he has the look of an innocent man?"

"I'm sure I wouldn't know, Aunt."

"Then there's Cook. She went to see Edward without being summoned. There has to be something in that."

"Yes, but what?"

"It's just odd. She's the cook, he was the master, and there's nothing to link them beyond that."

"Apart from her son," said Jane.

"Ah yes… he served under Edward during the War. Could it be anything to do with that?"

"I've no idea."

"I wonder…"

"Wonder what?"

Kate looked up ahead. They were approaching the Linton estate.

"I wonder if it has any bearing on Timothy and Edward's argument the evening before Edward's death."

Eighteen

Before any kind of normality had time to re-establish itself at Linton Hall, Kate and Jane went to the kitchen. Here they found Cook with her back to them tending some pots on the range set into the chimney, unaware of their arrival.

Despite being there on important business, Kate took a moment to admire the sizeable space with its freestanding dresser, open shelves, cupboards, pots hanging from hooks, and the large wooden table showing evidence of food preparation.

She loved a good kitchen.

"Sorry to trouble you again, Cook," she eventually said. "We're just back from the service."

Cook turned and, on seeing them, dried her hands on a cloth.

"A sad business, madam. Did it go well?"

"Yes, it did – despite the police being in church."

"Oh... is there something I can do for you?"

Kate took a moment to find the best way forward.

"I fear an innocent person might be hanged for murder."

Cook's face turned pale.

"That would be terrible, madam."

"You went to see Edward in the library. It's time to explain."

"I really don't have anything more to say."

"Cook, I'm not the police, but sometimes justice needs a helping hand. Are you willing to tell us what you know?"

"As I said before, he wanted something arranged."

"What specifically?"

"The food. He wanted me to do something different."

"You mentioned something about beef or duck. Could you elaborate?"

"I'm not sure what you mean."

"You went to see his lordship. Obviously, there had been an earlier conversation regarding beef or duck. Could you tell us why you went to see him again."

"It was a change to the plans... for today. I needed his final say on it."

Jane stepped in. "Was it something special for guests coming back after Lord George Linton's service?"

"Yes."

"So, what did Edward have in mind?"

"Um, well... I can't recall exactly."

125

Kate wasn't happy.

"Come on, Cook. Preparing meals is your field of expertise. You'll have assessed any requests with one eye on what the pantry held. Unless you placed an order in the village? That's easily checked."

Cook look flustered.

"There's no need to check. There was no order placed."

"So, everything needed was already in the house."

"Yes."

"And yet you're unable to recall the details. That doesn't seem very likely, does it."

Cook looked defeated, and Kate felt sympathy for her – but she continued all the same.

"What do you think Scotland Yard will make of all this? Once Inspector Ridley catches up with the matter of beef or duck, he'll come asking the same questions. You do know that, don't you? You do understand that should you suddenly avail him with full details, I'll be duty bound to let him know you've made it up to protect yourself. Or possibly to protect someone else."

"But I've done nothing wrong."

"Mrs Parker, the police have a habit of arresting people who confound the course of justice."

Jane stepped in again.

"Could your little chat with Edward have related to another matter?"

Cook's face flushed. Her eyes showed fear.

"How so, your ladyship?"

"Are you aware that Mr Lawson argued with Edward over a matter relating to the War?"

"No."

"Your son served under Edward, didn't he. What do you think this argument might've been about?"

"I've no idea, I'm sure," said Cook, close to tears. "I really don't wish to discuss any of this at all."

"Very well," said Kate, "but wouldn't it be terrible for the wrong person to hang and for you to be jailed for protecting the real killer?"

"I assure you I would never do that."

"Your son was a hero," said Jane. "We know you're very proud of him and his fine reputation."

Cook sniffed.

"You'll have seen stones for the Lintons in the graveyard today. My son's stone is in Belgium. He served under Edward and was killed running a top-secret communication. He was a very brave lad."

"Of course he was," said Kate. "A credit to his family and our beloved country. Above all things, he understood duty. We can only hope that when duty calls, each of us will rise to the occasion."

With that, she and Jane left the kitchen and made their way along the hallway.

"She's hiding something," said Jane.

"Agreed," said Kate.

Nineteen

Just before lunch, Jane was in her aunt's room, sitting on the edge of the bed, while Kate stood at the window, from where she could see Oliver, below on the terrace, no doubt thinking about things.

"I can't say this draughty window is as impressive as the main one in St Luke's," said Kate, turning to face her niece.

"Yes, it was beautiful with the sun coming through, wasn't it," said Jane. "What a brilliant way to deliver the recorded messages of the Bible to those unable to read."

"Pardon?"

"Their original purpose – to depict biblical messages to the illiterate during the Middle Ages."

"Yes, well, I wish we could gain a similar clarity with this murder business. I just hope Scotland Yard's man gets the killer sooner rather than later."

Jane came to the window. Below, Victoria came out to stand with Oliver. They were soon talking.

"Do you have doubts about Inspector Ridley?" Jane asked.

"No," said Kate.

"But you're still worried there's a chance of things going wrong?"

"Yes – after all, what do we know for certain?"

Jane thought for a moment.

"We know Pritchard saw Edward alive. Then, soon after, Edward was killed by an unknown hand. After that, Cook came along to see him. Then you went to the library to deliver that letter. Between Pritchard's and Cook's visits, only a limited number of people had a chance to go in unseen."

"Yes," said Kate. "Bartholomew Grantley returned from fishing early. Oliver stayed on at the river, but we only have his word for it. Victoria and Charlotte were in the blue drawing room. Timothy Lawson was in the billiards room. Margaret was in the music room. Florence was asleep upstairs. The thing is, most people lack an alibi."

"Yes, they do."

"Thank goodness you and I were together, Jane."

"If we look at the strongest motive, it gives us Oliver. He had everything to gain. If it's someone else, we'd need to dig deeper. I doubt Inspector Ridley would approve though."

There was a knock at the door.

Jane crossed the room to open it.

"Hello, Cook," she said, somewhat surprised. "Do come in."

Cook looked straight past Jane to Kate.

"Mrs Forbes, you know how precious my son's memory is to me."

"Of course I do. He was a brave lad. Please come in."

As Cook did so, Jane closed the door.

"He died running top-secret information."

"Yes, a noble cause."

Cook hesitated.

"What is it?" Kate asked gently.

"I don't know if I can…"

"If there's something you know that might cast light on recent events, you must tell us."

"My son…"

"Cook, a life is at stake."

"I got left this."

She withdrew a small buff envelope from the pocket of her apron and handed it to Kate. There was just one word scrawled on it: 'Cook'.

Kate peeked inside.

"A note?"

"It's why I went to the library. It was slipped under the kitchen door."

Kate carefully removed the note, touching only the edges. Despite the bad handwriting, it was easy enough to read.

"Well," she said a few moments later. "This puts things in a new light."

"I was hoping it could remain a secret," said Cook. "I didn't want everyone seeing it."

"I'm afraid we're beyond that point," said Kate.

She handed the note to Jane and went out onto the landing. Next, it was down the stairs and into the foyer. There, she encountered a constable.

"Would you kindly get Inspector Ridley. I'll be in my room. Tell him it's important."

Two minutes later, the inspector entered Kate's room. The constable was behind him but remained at the door.

"What's all this about?" Ridley demanded. "I don't take kindly to being summoned. And what's Mrs Parker doing here?"

For a moment, Kate almost faltered in the face of the inspector's ire. But this was no time for self-doubt.

"It's about Cook's dear son, Reginald. During the War, he was Edward's batman. He died bravely, carrying a top-secret message. Or so we thought."

Jane handed over the envelope.

"This explains why Cook went to see Edward," she said. "There's almost certainly no chance of fingerprints."

Ridley frowned as he accepted it. He then spent the next few moments handling it carefully while studying the contents.

"I see," he said finally.

"Yes, inspector," said Kate. "That dear boy still died heroically. But for no good reason."

Ridley returned the note to the envelope and placed it in his inside pocket.

"This certainly changes things."

"My thoughts exactly," said Kate. "The thing is, someone in our midst has committed murder and attempted to lay the blame at Cook's door."

"Let me stop you there, Mrs Forbes. Thanks to this note, Cook, you are most definitely under suspicion for the murder of Lord Edward Linton."

"Yes," said Kate, "but we must also ask ourselves has someone written it to cover for their own actions?"

"Just leave it with me," said the inspector.

"The handwriting's disguised," Jane added. "I'd say whoever wrote it used their left hand. Or, if they're left-handed…"

"Yes, I'd worked that out, thank you."

"Good," said Kate. "So, what's our next move?"

Ridley's brow shot up.

"I don't know about you, Mrs Forbes, but *my* next move is to find out who wrote this note."

Kate sighed.

"This no doubt relates to what I partly overheard after dinner the night before the murder."

Ridley looked perplexed.

"What exactly did you overhear?"

"Timothy and Edward were having words about the War. It's possible it related to this matter."

Ridley shook his head.

"Is there any point to anyone signing a statement? Half the facts are left out. Right, I need to find out more. Constable, get everyone in the living room, including the staff."

Twenty

The entire household had assembled in the living room. Some were seated, others stood, but all faced Inspector Ridley who was standing by the fireplace.

"A note has come into my possession," he began. "It relates to the death of the cook's son during the War."

He held the note up in one hand, the envelope in the other.

"Now, someone in this room wrote this note and slid it under the kitchen door. I need to know who."

There was a general muttering but nothing in the way of an answer.

Ridley wasn't impressed.

"May I remind you that this is a murder investigation. Despite our best efforts, the crime scene has revealed no fingerprints or any other incriminating evidence, and no one saw or heard anything vital. This note could be instrumental in bringing the killer to justice, so ask yourselves – do you have any idea who might've written it."

"What's in the note?" Bartholomew Grantley asked.

"Whoever wrote it is well aware of its contents," said Ridley.

"Well, that's me out of your equation then, inspector. I haven't the foggiest idea."

Ridley glanced over at the cook.

"I was hoping to spare Mrs Parker the distress of hearing it all again. However, the gist of the note is at odds with the established story of her son's death. Up until now, the belief has been that he died running a top-secret message. This note says he died running for a bottle of brandy."

"Under orders from Edward?" said Oliver, aghast.

"Yes, quite so."

Once again, a general muttering passed around the room. This was clearly a revelation to most of those gathered.

"Well, begging Cook's pardon and all that," said Bartholomew, "but doesn't this give her a motive to kill Edward?"

Kate looked across the room to Cook, whose face was ashen.

"Somebody give Cook a chair," she said. "Please."

Timothy Lawson got up and slid his across to Cook, who was helped onto it by the maid.

"So Cook had a reason to want Edward dead," Sir Charles uttered.

Kate baulked at that.

"Wishing someone dead and killing them are two different things, Charles Sutton!"

There was a collective 'ooh' at Kate's deliberate slight.

"Of course, my dear," said Sir Charles with a smile.

"Cook treasures her son's reputation," Kate reminded them all. "I'm surprised she didn't burn the rotten note!"

"Perhaps her conscience got the better of her," said Bartholomew, before turning to Jane. "You're not upset by war tales, are you?"

"No more than any other sane person. My brother Alexander fought throughout 1918 as a young second lieutenant. We talked about some of his experiences."

"Alright, let's have a bit of order," said Ridley. "I'll ask again – does anyone know who wrote this note?"

Faced with silence, he turned to Oliver.

"How about you, Lord Linton? I assume you're using the title?"

"I'm not responsible for tradition, inspector."

"Did you write the note to Cook?"

Oliver looked frustrated.

"Until just now, I'd never heard this new version of the story. Far be it from me to tell you how to proceed, but you'll need to find those who did."

"Your brother never mentioned it?"

"My brother never spoke of the War. At least not to me."

"He didn't need to tell Timothy Lawson," said Sir Charles. "He was there, weren't you, old boy."

All turned to Timothy.

"I resent having fingers pointed at me!" he hooted.

"Alright," said Ridley. "But Mr Lawson, it's strange that you should be arguing with Edward about the War the night before his death, then something relating to the War turns up in this note, and then Edward's found dead."

Timothy wasn't having any of it. He turned to Bartholomew.

"You're far more likely to have killed him. That New York business upset you badly."

Ridley's eyes widened.

"What New York business?"

"This is all utter rot!" Bartholomew insisted.

"Right," said Ridley, "I'll be interviewing you all again, one at a time – starting with Mr Lawson, Mr Grantley and Lord Oliver Linton. And this time, I want to know everything!"

Ridley marched off in the direction of the study, while the constable ushered the three named men in the same direction.

"Well, I never," said Sir Charles. "All three of 'em look guilty."

"Don't be so dramatic, Charles," said Florence. "It's merely a formality."

With much to discuss, Kate and Jane made their excuses and returned to Kate's room. Once there, Kate wasted no time in getting to the point.

"What do you think, Jane? Oliver swears he never knew that dreadful story."

"He could be telling the truth."

"Possibly, but I don't believe Cook's a killer, and neither am I convinced of Oliver's guilt."

"Is this intuition, Aunt Kate?"

"Henry often said there's no room for intuition in deciding a person's fate, but that it's not a bad place to start when seeking the evidence to do so."

"Are you suggesting we should act further?"

"Yes, but I'm not sure how."

Jane considered it.

"Wouldn't Inspector Ridley take a dim view of us continuing to help him?"

"We've done nothing to hinder the inspector. We've simply explored alternative routes to justice. Assuming he reaches the correct conclusion, there's no reason for him to even suspect we've been at work."

"He's a detective from Scotland Yard, Aunt. If he doesn't detect us continuing to investigate his case, he can't be much good."

"Jane. the only thing that matters is seeing justice done. It shouldn't matter who cracks the case."

"It might matter to Inspector Ridley. Professional pride and all that."

"I'm sure he'll arrive at the truth long before we do, but regardless of that, let's give it our best shot, shall we?"

"Yes, Aunt."

Twenty-One

Kate and Jane were alone in the dining room enjoying freshly baked bread with cheddar cheese, cold ham, leftover boiled potatoes and a spoonful of Green Label Indian mango chutney.

"The question before us," said Kate between mouthfuls, "is who knew the true War story?"

"Cook knew," said Jane. "Although, she says she only found out when she read the note."

"Yes, well, we can't rule out prior knowledge. It's possible she wrote the note herself after Edward's death to deflect the blame elsewhere."

"Either way, it's not clear cut."

"No, it's not," agreed Kate, "although I haven't lost sight of Cook more than likely being innocent."

Jane nodded.

"I feel the same way."

"So, what else do we have?"

"Quite a bit," said Jane. "Timothy Lawson served with Edward during the War. He knew the true story. And he argued with Edward. *And* he was alone in the billiards room which is just along the hallway from the library."

"Did I hear my name?" said Timothy entering the dining room.

"Ah, Mr Lawson," said Kate. "We were just speculating. That note was written by someone who knew the true War story."

"Yes, I knew it, but as I mentioned earlier, I didn't write the note."

At the sideboard, he put some bread and ham on a plate then then took a seat at the table.

"Ridley's through with Oliver," he continued. "He's got Barty in there now. My turn next. It's like being summoned by the headmaster."

"You *are* aware that I overheard you arguing with Edward the night before his death?"

"I do wish you'd stay out of it, Mrs Forbes. You'll get me hanged."

"You were arguing about this War business. I heard quite a bit as I was passing by."

"Oh?" said a constable from the doorway. "Walking slowly, were we?"

"Kindly keep out of it, constable," said Kate. "This is a private conversation."

"I'm just keeping an eye on Mr Lawson. We don't want him nipping off before the inspector's had a word with him."

"I think some fresh air, Jane," said Kate rising from her unfinished lunch. She turned to the constable. "I trust that's in order?"

"As you wish, madam."

"One thing before you go," said Timothy. "While you two ladies plot to convict me of murder, you might want to take something into account. Both Barty and Sir Charles knew the true War story *before* the note surfaced."

"Mr Grantley and Sir Charles?" said Kate. "Who told them?"

"I did. In strict confidence, mind – but either of them could be your note-writer."

"You were in the same regiment as Edward, but you disliked him," said Jane.

"We all did."

"Edward served his country," said Kate.

"Hah! He was so incompetent he was practically working for the enemy."

"At least he made something of himself," said Kate. "After the War he went to Paris. Charlotte says he found his place in life."

"Nonsense. Charlotte's obsessed with the arts scene. She even paid for Victoria to accompany her to Paris this summer in the hope of becoming inspired. Look how that turned out. Trust me, Edward was losing money. Had it not been for his allowance, he'd have gone broke."

"Bartholomew seemed to have time for him," Jane pointed out. "At least up until he mentioned going to New York."

*

A short while later, Kate and Jane were walking down to the river. Here, on the footpath, away from prying eyes and ears, they were able to speculate further.

"Can we believe Timothy Lawson?" Kate wondered.

"I'm not sure," said Jane. "What if he were blackmailing Edward for some reason. His war record, for example. Then again, if Timothy was after Edward's money, why kill him?"

"Anger?" suggested Kate.

"Surely, that's Cook's motive."

"Yes, possibly…"

At the riverbank, they took in the Arun's meandering course as it made its way down to the village.

"It's lovely," said Jane. "So peaceful."

Kate peered into the water… and there! A glint of scale and fin.

"I wonder if this is where Oliver and Bartholomew were fishing. It looks like a good spot."

"Yes, Barty…" Jane mused. "We should have a word with him. And Sir Charles too. Seeing as they knew the true War story."

"Yes, alright," said Kate. "First chance we get."

Twenty-Two

Fresh from their walk, Kate and Jane sought refuge in the quiet blue drawing room. However, they had barely sat down when Bartholomew Grantley stopped by the open door.

"Oh, hello. I thought it might be empty."

"Come in, Bartholomew," said Kate. "We won't bite."

He came in but remained on his feet.

"Strange times," he mused.

"I expect you've just come from your chat with Inspector Ridley," said Kate.

"Spying on me, eh?"

"You came from the direction of the study."

"Ah… well, yes, he went over every aspect of it with me. When did I leave Oliver? Did I see anyone else at the river, or on my way back, or when I approached or entered the house? Have you ever been asked the same questions

145

over and over? I've a good mind to pack my bags and leave."

"You'll only draw attention to yourself," said Jane. "There's always the assumption that the first to flee has the most to fear from the police."

"With respect, Lady Jane, that's nonsense."

"We might be able to help you," said Kate.

Bartholomew viewed them both with suspicion.

"How?"

"Edward was your second cousin," said Jane, "but you had no meaningful relationship with him until you met up in Paris a couple of years ago. Did you become good friends?"

"I'm not sure that's relevant."

"It is," said Kate. "Your life could be at stake."

"Look, what's this about? How can you help me?"

"By establishing the facts."

"I thought that was Ridley's job."

Kate puffed out her cheeks.

"We're not convinced of Oliver's or Cook's guilt."

"I see. So, you think it was Timothy Lawson."

"Not necessarily," said Jane.

"Oh, so you're looking to lay the blame at my door instead. That's hardly helping me."

"If you're innocent, you have nothing to fear," said Kate.

"Nothing to fear? How many men down the years have been told that before finding themselves in front of a judge donning the black hat?"

"How would you describe the health of Edward's business in Paris?" asked Jane.

Bartholomew sighed.

"It had potential."

"Mr Lawson says it was a failure."

"I'm not interested in anything he has to say. Edward bought and sold paintings. He may have lost a little money but it's not a crime if you can pay your debts."

"Did you ever seek to work with him?" Kate asked.

"I've been through all this with the police. Apart from the occasional brief chat, there was nothing concrete between Edward and me."

"Then why react so badly to his New York plans?"

Bartholomew's eyes flared with indignation.

"You have no right to question me!" he said before marching off.

*

A few minutes later, as Kate and Jane wondered what their next step might be, they had another visitor.

"Not interrupting, am I?" Sir Charles enquired at the door.

"Come in, come in," said Kate.

"No, no, I was on my way to the billiards room. I just wondered what you two were up to, that's all."

"Not much," said Kate. "We were asking young Bartholomew some questions when he took flight."

"Ah yes, I saw him storm out for a walk. I dare say he'll find some trees to shout at. One thing's for certain – that New York business upset him. Don't ask me for details though. He's not the type to tell tales."

"Talking of tales," said Kate. "When did you learn of the War story?"

"That old nonsense? I don't recall."

"Timothy Lawson says he told you."

"Did he? Yes, possibly." Sir Charles then laughed. "Oh alright, I admit it. I didn't like Edward, so I killed him."

Kate was perplexed. "Really?"

"Yes, I've killed dozens of rotters all over Sussex. Well, you can't leave it to the law, can you? They always make a hash of it."

"I thought you were in the Red Lion at the time of the murder?"

"Ah, so I was. It can't have been me then. Better luck next time, ladies."

"Really, Charles…"

"Do feel free to interrogate me again. It's jolly good fun."

"Sir Charles?" Jane enquired. "Before you go, would you describe Charlotte as a woman of integrity?"

Sir Charles' cheery disposition evaporated.

"Well now, Lady Jane. For me, she likes to be seen as a living champion of a movement she's ideologically not part of. If you can find any integrity in that, good luck."

Kate waited for him to disappear down the hall before commenting.

"Charlotte?"

"Yes, there's something there," said Jane. "I'm just not sure what."

"Well, all we can say for certain is that someone wanted Edward dead."

"Someone who stood to gain," Jane added.

"It's still possible Cook killed Edward and faked the note," said Kate. "Even if we'd prefer not to believe it."

Jane considered it.

"Elizabeth Parker, known to all as Cook. Her son died during the War. A hero's death. Except now we know he died on a fool's errand. She had the motive, the murder weapon was already in the room, and with Edward drunk, she had a clear opportunity. The question is, how can we prove she had no idea of the true War story, and was therefore never in a position to write the note?"

Kate shrugged.

"She's been at Linton Hall a long time. Had she known, why continue to work here? Surely, she'd have left long ago."

"Let's stay with our idea of Cook being innocent," said Jane. "So, she receives a note from an unknown hand…

the contents disturb her… she decides to confront the cause of her son's needless death…"

"Yes, and next thing we know, Edward's dead. It's not a very favourable picture, is it."

"No, it's not, but there's another aspect to all this. If she killed Edward, why not claim it as justice for her son?"

"How do you mean?"

"I mean if she's the killer, then we're looking at a woman who praises her son's bravery to the heavens and yet hides her own actions behind a cowardly, demeaning lie."

"Good point, Jane. It's tempting to think her pride in her son might have compelled her to see it through with a degree of courage. Not just during the act, but in taking responsibility."

"It's not proof of her innocence," said Jane, "but I still lean towards her not being the killer."

"Perhaps we should continue to look elsewhere then."

"If we're to protect her, then yes, we should."

Twenty-Three

A few minutes later, Florence Nettleton appeared at the blue drawing room door.

"How timely, Florrie," said Kate. "We're just going through the suspects."

"Oh, am I one?"

But Kate could now see that Florence wasn't alone. Coming in behind her were Charlotte, Margaret and Victoria.

"Ladies," said Kate. "How lovely."

"So, who are the suspects?" asked Margaret.

"According to Scotland Yard, most of us," said Kate.

"But what do *you* think," said Florence.

"Well... the culprit is either Cook or someone trying to lay the blame on her. If the latter, then who?"

"Poor Cook," said Florence. "I don't mind answering questions."

"No, this doesn't apply to you, Florrie," said Kate. "You're a good egg."

"No," said Florence. "I shouldn't be above suspicion. None of us should."

"Well… alright," said Kate. "Where were you at the time of the incident?"

"In my room, asleep."

"Do you sleepwalk?"

"I don't know. Mind you, if I did, wouldn't people have noticed before now?"

"Florrie, assuming Edward was going to sell the house, you were likely to become homeless."

"Is that the motive?" Florence asked.

"Yes, that's the motive. Or at least one of them."

"Isn't it the same motive Pritchard might have harboured?"

"It is," said Jane. "It's also a potential motive for Oliver, Charlotte and Cook."

"So, what does that tell us?" Victoria asked.

"Good question," said Jane. "It's a motive that rules out anyone not on that list."

"There would be other motives though?" said Margaret.

"Yes, greed would be another," said Jane. "That would be a matter of looking at who had the most to gain."

"That's Oliver," said Kate, although she didn't feel happy about saying so.

"And Charlotte, of course," Florence added. "Sorry, Charlotte."

"It's no bother, Aunt Florence."

"No bother?" said Kate, surprised at Charlotte's indifference. "Please don't be offended, but you received a very generous allowance from your father. With Edward taking the reins, you were likely to get practically nothing. As motives go, that's quite a strong one."

"Are we saying Edward lacked generosity?" Victoria asked.

"Very much so. But with Oliver taking over, all's well again."

"Yes, Oliver's a generous spirit," said Florence. "A chip off the old block."

"But what of you, Victoria?" said Jane. "You say you first met Edward in Paris."

"That's right. I was with Charlotte."

"Do you recall the second time you met him?"

Victoria seemed surprised.

"The second time?"

"Was that also in Paris?"

"It's possible we saw him there a second time. I don't recall."

"No," said Charlotte. "We saw him just the once. At that gallery. Don't you remember?"

"You're right," Victoria confirmed. "We saw him just the once."

"But what of you, Lady Jane?" Charlotte asked. "Have you accounted for your own movements?"

"I was with Aunt Kate. Unless Inspector Ridley suspects us of working together, we shouldn't be on his list."

"Quite right," said Florence.

"It raises the idea though, doesn't it," said Jane. "Of two people working together. Charlotte and Victoria... you were in this room at the time of the murder. I know it's indelicate, but isn't there the possibility of you two co-operating?"

"That's quite fanciful," said Charlotte.

"You were opposite the library," Jane pointed out. "Getting there and back unseen wouldn't have been much of an issue."

"Especially if one played lookout for the other?" said Kate.

Charlotte shrugged.

"We were simply passing the time of day."

"It's amazing what friends will do for each other," said Jane. "How long have you known Victoria?"

"We met at a garden party in... June, was it?"

"The end of May," said Victoria.

Charlotte nodded.

"We've been close ever since."

"Hmm," said Kate. "And what about Margaret? You were playing piano in the music room. That's just a few steps down the hallway."

Margaret looked shocked.

"The piano would have fallen silent," she said.

"You were practising," Kate pointed out. "It's only natural to play for a few minutes and then pause for a time."

"That's true," said Florence, "but Margaret's in my care and I can tell you she's not the type to go around killing people."

"Then who is?" said Jane. "Who stood to gain enough to kill for it?"

There was a moment of reflection before Victoria uttered a name.

"Oliver."

"Unless," said Jane, "it's someone who gained by preventing an action. For example, Edward's New York plans upset Bartholomew Grantley."

"Then again," said Kate, "Timothy Lawson is linked to this new version of the War story."

"And what about Charles?" said Florence. "What if he came back from the pub, committed the deed, and nipped out again?"

"After three pints of beer, three double whiskies and a pie?" said Kate.

"Kate, dear, we only have his word for that. Who's to say he wasn't stone cold sober?"

Victoria sighed.

"So, it comes down to Cook, and whether she wrote the note."

"That's the heart of it," said Kate. "If Cook knew the true War story, she had plenty of time to write the note after Edward's death to muddy the waters."

"What's your next move then?" Florence asked.

"That's a very good question," said Kate.

Twenty-Four

Kate and Jane stepped out of the blue drawing room into the hallway opposite the library. There were just three rooms farther along: the music room on the left, the study on the right and, at the end of the corridor, the billiards room.

It was the study door they were soon outside.

Kate gave a light knock.

"Come in," came the reply from within.

She pushed the door open and took in a rare view of the room. This had long been George's domain and not somewhere he'd generally invite others.

The centrepiece was a Victorian oak desk with green leather inlay. With a matching leather chair behind it and two plain wooden chairs in front, it stood on a large red and gold Persian rug which covered over half the polished wooden floor. Beyond the desk, a large sash window overlooked the front of the house, perhaps affording his lordship the opportunity to look out for arrivals before Pritchard came knocking to announce them. And here, Inspector Ridley stood with his back to them, doing likewise. He only turned when Jane closed the door.

"Oh… I was expecting a constable."

"Sorry for the intrusion," said Kate, "but Jane and I have been thinking about the case. More minds quicken the workload, wouldn't you agree."

"Possibly not, but carry on."

"We owe you an apology. We poked our noses in where they weren't wanted and got nowhere."

"Don't tell me, you failed to identify who wrote the note, which means you can't identify the killer."

"Yes, so if you've been troubled by our presence, we're stepping down."

"I'm glad to hear it. I don't approve of amateurs getting involved in police matters."

Kate indicated to Jane that they should withdraw, but Ridley wasn't finished.

"There's just one thing," he said. "I'm stumped too."

"Oh?" said Kate.

"The cook lacks an alibi. Unless it can be proven she had no knowledge of the true War story, then she has to be the most likely suspect. It's just that I don't buy it."

He took the chair behind the desk and indicated that Kate and Jane might like to sit opposite.

They did so.

"But that's only the half of it," he continued. "Whether Cook knew the true War story has no bearing on my duty to look at the other suspects. If she's innocent, then someone in this house killed Edward Linton and sought to blame her. Just how I prove that though…"

"We also lean towards Cook being innocent," said Kate. "But it's no more than a feeling."

"She's lived here a long time," said Ridley. "Was she really waiting for Edward to return from Paris? From what I understand, he visited Linton Hall a few times over the years. If she knew the true story, why wait until now?"

"It's tempting to rule her out," said Jane, "but she had the clearest of motives and the opportunity to commit the crime."

Ridley nodded.

"Which brings us back to her being the most likely murderer."

"Poor Cook," said Kate. "The prosecution at her trial would have a compelling case."

"Agreed," said Ridley. "It doesn't look good for her. That said, whichever way we look at it, the killer had to know the War story."

"Timothy Lawson was in the army with Edward," said Jane. "He knew it."

"Yes," said Ridley, "but he says he told it to both Sir Charles Sutton and Bartholomew Grantley."

"Sir Charles has an alibi," said Kate.

"Yes, but Lawson and Grantley don't," said Ridley. "And then there's Oliver Linton. He also lacks an alibi."

"He says he didn't know the true version of the story," said Kate.

"I know, but I have to ask myself – do I believe him? That said, the opportunity to commit the crime is the weakest part of the case against him. How well he knows this place is one thing, but no one saw him come back."

"The easiest thing," said Jane, "would be to arrest Cook and have done with it."

"You don't know me, Lady Jane, but justice comes first. It's never out of my thoughts that the real killer might want me to go with the easiest solution."

"Yes, indeed," said Kate.

"We did give some thought to Bartholomew," said Jane. "What if he had a business association with Edward? And what if Edward going to New York changed things? Then again, Barty's an able man. I'm sure it wouldn't have been the end of the world."

Ridley shrugged.

"There was nothing among Edward's papers – although he might have destroyed anything relating to an earlier arrangement. There's also Timothy Lawson. He's involved in the family's financial affairs. Perhaps Edward was going to throw him overboard."

"Timothy argued with Edward the night before the murder," said Kate.

"He has a temper," said Jane. "What if he acted on the spur of the moment? He's smart. Writing the note would point the blame elsewhere."

"His temper, eh?" said Ridley. "It's true he doesn't hide that. It's possible he acted in anger, but we'd need to find the reason. It would've been something big, something that Edward said that changed things for Lawson, and not to his advantage."

"Most likely something to do with money," said Kate.

"There's also Charlotte Linton," said Jane. "Her allowance fears were allayed by Edward's death. Then again, was she in a position to commit the crime?"

"There's also Margaret Tavistock and Victoria Eustace," said Ridley, "but they barely knew Edward. Other than that, Pritchard stood to lose his home, but so did Mrs Nettleton. Of course, Pritchard was the last to see Edward alive."

"So, who had a realistic opportunity to commit the crime?" said Jane.

"Too many," said Ridley. "Bartholomew Grantley came back earlier than Oliver Linton, so it's possible. Margaret Tavistock was playing the piano, which is close to the library. Then there's Timothy Lawson playing billiards, so he's not far from the library either. Then there's Charlotte Linton and Victoria Eustace playing chess and knitting. As for Sir Charles Sutton and Florence Nettleton… I don't see it. No, I won't act just yet. There's something I'm missing. It'll turn up though. Killers always leave clues. You just have to work out where to find them."

"Well, thank you for seeing us," said Kate.

"Not at all. Sometimes it's good to talk things through."

Kate raised an eyebrow.

"Even with amateurs?"

Ridley declined to comment.

A few moments later, in the hallway, Jane wondered.

"I suppose we'll still keep our eyes and ears open?"

"I think we must," said Kate. "Stepping down might not be the right thing to do, after all."

"That's what I was thinking," said Jane. "You never know, the answer might be closer than we think."

Twenty-Five

Kate was late coming down to dinner. The first gong had sounded a while ago and the second was due shortly. It had been a long afternoon.

Approaching the red drawing room, she heard Jane and Charlotte just beyond the door. Rather than enter, she held back for a moment.

"It's entirely understandable," said Jane, "but are you sure you didn't see anything unusual? It might be something that's occurred to you since."

"No," said Charlotte. "I've already told you I was with Victoria. We saw nothing."

"So, you never left the room, even for a few minutes?"

"I don't like being questioned, Lady Jane. I was with Victoria when Pritchard came along with Edward's coffee. We remained together until your aunt knocked that vase over."

"Ah, there you all are," said Kate on entering. Everyone had already gathered within, many armed with a fortifying glass of sherry or gin.

"Aunt Kate," said Jane. "The second gong's about to sound."

"My watch stopped," said Kate. "I thought I had more time between gongs – but don't let me interrupt you."

Kate didn't want to get in Jane's way. Progress might be hindered. With a plan to listen in first, she surveyed the room.

Once again, the men looked smart in dinner jackets and ties. As for the women, Margaret looked elegant in black taffeta, as did Jane in her midnight blue silk dress, while Charlotte opted for another strange long jumper, this time in dark purple with cigarette ash down the front. Victoria, meanwhile, looked lovely in dark green satin – a dress choice she was discussing with Florence and Sir Charles.

"It's so important to know the latest fashions," she told them.

At this, Sir Charles huffed and strode away.

"Take no notice of him," said Kate, moving in. "Charles believes they perfected clothes in Queen Victoria's reign."

"Mrs Forbes," said Oliver, coming over to join them. "Sherry?"

"A small one, thank you."

"Of course, change is relentless," said Florence. "I mean the pace of modern life… well, it's so dizzying. When I was a girl, we didn't have people whizzing around in sporty motorcars, flying off to Paris, or making telephone calls to who-knows-where."

A glass of sherry reached Kate's hand.

"Thank you, Oliver."

The conversation on the changing world continued between Florence and Victoria, but without Kate's full attention. Her ears were straining to listen in on Jane and Charlotte.

"Kate?" said Florence.

"Pardon?"

"Motor cars. Don't you agree?"

"Oh, er, yes…"

It was no use; she couldn't hear Jane and Charlotte properly. What if the fish were wriggling off the hook?

She made her excuses and turned away.

"Don't mind me," she said, stepping into Jane and Charlotte's sphere.

She just needed a clever angle.

"I was just thinking of Christmas… in other parts of the world. Paris, for example."

Yes, Paris would be a worthwhile avenue.

"I'd imagine it's lovely there," she continued. "Of course, it's where Bartholomew established a closer relationship with Edward."

Kate was pleased with her approach work, but Charlotte glanced across the room to where her second cousin Bartholomew was now in a corner talking with Sir Charles.

"Yes, that's right," she replied in advance of her gaze returning to Kate.

"Bartholomew's a businessman. Do you know if he and Edward had any joint plans?"

"No, sorry, Mrs Forbes. There was some talk of them possibly doing something together, but I don't think anything came of it."

"Interesting," said Kate, although any follow up was curtailed by the sound of the second gong.

As Charlotte headed for the dining room, Jane leaned in close to her aunt.

"Paris eh? Exactly what I've been thinking."

*

At the dinner table, it was immediately evident that the head of the household's chair would remain empty.

Sir Charles pointed to Oliver, who was in his usual seat.

"Shouldn't you be sitting there, old boy?"

"That's not very helpful, Sir Charles," said Charlotte.

"Perhaps in a few days," said Oliver.

"Now I understand King Arthur," said Florence. "A round table has a lot to offer."

"Round table, my foot," said Sir Charles. "There'd still be one of 'em with a bigger chair."

"Might we speak about something else?" Oliver requested.

"As you wish," said Timothy Lawson. "Lady Jane, you came here to be introduced to Edward. Had he lived, you might be with him now, hurtling towards a lifeless marriage. Do you ever ponder the vagaries of Fate?"

"Introductions hardly form a binding contract," Jane replied.

"I'm glad to hear it. I like a girl who knows her own mind."

"Has anyone been to Scotland?" Kate asked, seeking to change the subject. "I don't know why I asked that. Perhaps it's this cold weather we're having."

"I love Scotland, and it's not always cold," said Bartholomew. "I was up there during the summer. There was a festival in Edinburgh but, best of all, some friends took me out to play golf. What a good game it is. Anyone else play?"

"I used to play," said Sir Charles. "And I do believe the game originated in Scotland. Not too sure of the history though."

Kate, Victoria and Margaret all looked to Jane, who had somehow become the *de facto* historian.

"Oh, I don't know much," she said, "apart from King James the Second of Scotland banning it because his men would play golf instead of practising archery."

"Oh really?" said Margaret. "How interesting."

"Yes," Jane continued, "I think it was James the Fourth who reinstated it. Perhaps for us ladies though, the most interesting thing I can tell you is that Mary, Queen of Scots is thought to be the first woman to be a devotee of the game. She learned to play during her childhood in France, which explains the word, 'caddie.' As a member of the French royal family, her clubs would have been carried by a military cadet."

"At last," said Sir Charles, "the evening has taken a pleasant turn."

Inspector Ridley strode in without a knock.

"Lord Linton, I have further questions for you. Would you mind…?"

Oliver sighed.

"Not now, inspector, surely?"

"I'm not satisfied with anything you've told me."

"This is too much. You have no evidence and, more to the point, I'm innocent."

"A jury might have something to say about that. You're the only one under this roof who gains. Now, shall we go to the study for a little chat?"

"I was just about to eat."

"We all have to miss the occasional meal, your lordship. Shall we…?"

A disturbed Oliver threw down his napkin and rose from the table.

"Do excuse me."

No sooner they'd left, Sir Charles tutted.

"Poor Oliver."

"I think it's appalling," said Charlotte.

"I agree," said Victoria.

"Unfortunately, our opinions count for nothing," said Florence.

Kate turned to Jane.

"The inspector was undecided earlier. Now it seems he's settled for an obvious motive. You know what that means…"

Twenty-Six

Kate and Jane were heading up the stairs after dinner.

"Whatever happens, we need to keep calm if we're to set the record straight," said Kate as they reached their landing.

"Agreed," said Jane. "I'm just not sure what our next move should be."

"Well, why don't we—"

But the sound of the gong interrupted their progress.

"What on earth's going on?" Kate wondered.

They turned and went back downstairs, where they found others milling about looking equally confused. Chief gong-basher Pritchard was meanwhile pointing to the hallway, from where Inspector Ridley could be heard.

"Could you all join me in the living room?" he asked.

They duly complied, finding Oliver already there, standing solemnly by the drawn curtains at the window.

Once everyone had settled, Ridley addressed them.

"A letter has come into my possession. I'd also say it's come at a very timely moment. I'd finished for the evening, but what do I find when I open the study door to leave? Mr Pritchard standing there holding an envelope with my name on it… an envelope he found on the table in this room. It was no doubt placed for him or another member of the staff to find when they stoked the fire."

Sir Charles tutted.

"People do seem to keep leaving pieces of paper lying around."

"Yes, well, this one may well change things," said Ridley.

"How so?" Kate enquired.

"Because when I opened it, there was a smaller envelope inside. This one, in fact." Ridley held it up for all to see. "It's addressed to Mr Grantley."

Bartholomew gasped.

"What? Who the blazes has been rifling through my belongings?"

"You'd do well to keep quiet, Mr Grantley. This doesn't look very good for you at all."

Bartholomew's face was ashen. The assembly meanwhile gawped at Ridley, wondering what might come next.

"This letter, addressed to Mr Grantley, was sent by Edward, the previous Lord Linton."

"The eighth Baron," said Sir Charles.

"Never mind the numbers. The letter concerns a business arrangement between sender and recipient."

"I'd really like that back," said Bartholomew. "It's private and confidential."

"Yes, Mr Grantley. It's also evidence in a murder investigation. Do you have anything to say about its contents?"

"What contents?" Sir Charles asked. "We haven't heard them yet."

"You might not hear them at all. Assuming Mr Grantley comes clean."

"I've nothing to hide," Bartholomew insisted. "It's a letter from Edward regarding a business deal concerning an art gallery."

"You were both about to sign a contract, Mr Grantley."

"Yes, and everything was going smoothly until the other day. Then we learned he was relocating to New York."

"In your view, what did that mean?"

"Well, it certainly didn't mean Edward and I were off to New York. No… it meant our deal was off."

"What exactly was this deal?"

"To set up shop in London."

"So… would I be right in thinking that Edward, as the new Lord Linton, was suddenly able to set himself up in New York without your help?"

"Yes."

"Destroying your chance to make a success of yourself in London?"

"Edward was to open doors that I couldn't."

"That's a motive for murder, Mr Grantley."

"I didn't kill him, inspector."

"Who do you think did then?"

"I've no idea."

"Mr Grantley, you've lied to the police in two interviews where you swore that you and Edward had no meaningful business dealings."

"Yes, but I didn't want to implicate myself. I hated Edward after being let down. To have the gallery open in New York instead of London, and for me to not be part of it…"

"After all the hard work you'd put in?"

"Yes."

"I've arranged for a car to take you to the police station in Littlehampton. I don't want you taking flight. You'll be held pending charges."

"You've got the wrong man, inspector. The person you want is whoever stole my letter. And we know who that was. Those two!"

Bartholomew was pointing unequivocally at Kate and Jane.

Kate was outraged.

"We'd never stoop that low."

"I'll get to the bottom of it in due course," said Ridley. "The fact is, Mr Grantley, no jury will side with someone who's knowingly lied to the police."

Bartholomew Grantley pushed past Timothy Lawson and ran for the door… only to crash into the constable placed just outside by Ridley.

"Trying to escape?" said the inspector. "That never reads well in court either."

"I'm innocent. Surely you can all see that?"

"You listen to me, young man," said Kate. "Despite your discourtesy, I'll look into this for you."

"You stay out of it, you mad old bat!"

Kate watched the constable dragging Bartholomew away.

"He's very fortunate," she said. "I shan't allow insults to cloud my judgement."

"You're almost there, inspector," said Jane. "As soon as you discover who took Barty's letter, you can be certain you've got the real killer."

"I'm sorry, Lady Jane, but you're wrong. I've got the right man," said Ridley before leaving the room.

"It all adds up," said Sir Charles. "Barty was due to set up a gallery with Edward in London, but then it's all cut short. With a title, Edward could set himself up in New York. There would be plenty of takers over there."

"It's the way of the world," said Victoria. "Barty needed Edward for his name. Barty himself is a good businessman but he's barely qualified to move in the best circles. He only got there through his mother marrying above her station. Really, it was generous of Edward to help him."

"What are you talking about?" said Timothy Lawson. "Barty was the brains. Without him, Edward was hopeless."

"That's an exaggeration," said Victoria.

"Is it? Did you know they met for the first time in years when Barty stopped him overpaying for some old tat."

"I really wouldn't know. I was in Paris with Charlotte. That's when I first met Edward. It was very brief, but he seemed to be in his element."

"Nonsense," said Timothy. "Edward didn't have a clue. He was lucky to have Barty as a second cousin."

"So, you're friends with Barty now, are you?" Sir Charles enquired.

"Can't stand him," said Timothy, "but that has nothing to do with setting the record straight."

"Well… we'll say goodnight," said Kate, tired of all the bickering.

"Yes," said Jane. "It's been another long day."

In the hallway, Kate turned for the foyer and stairs, but Jane had other ideas.

"I just want to take a quick look in the blue drawing room."

"Whatever for?"

"I'm not sure."

A moment later, they entered the room. It was empty.

"What are we doing, Jane?"

"I'm just… um…"

But Jane said no more, instead concentrating on certain odd activities, such as sitting at the table, and then going to the window and facing the room from there as if it might mean something.

Finally, she sighed.

"Sorry, Aunt." She glanced at the clock on the mantlepiece. "It's late."

"Yes, although I don't think I can sleep, Jane. Perhaps we could stay a bit longer and go over what we know."

Twenty-Seven

Kate went to the door and peered down the hallway. Everyone else was still in the living room.

"It does look bad for Barty," said Jane.

"There's an awful snobbishness going on there," said Kate, keeping her voice down. "He may not be from the highest echelons of society, but he's bright."

She stepped back into the room.

"I agree," said Jane. "I think Edward's lack of success in Paris meant he needed a safe pair of hands to run the show in London. And who better than a keen and able businessman from the family's distant lower ranks?"

"I have to say it rings true," said Kate.

"Yes, but then, Edward, suddenly a baron, sensed a fresh opportunity on the other side of the Atlantic, where he believed he'd easily find a home without having Barty dragging up his Paris failings should he choose to."

"Yes, I can see that. Very much so. With the sale of Linton Hall, he'd have set himself up very nicely."

"It's not hard to imagine," said Jane. "Taking on a plush apartment in the best part of town, renting the best business premises, hiring genuine art experts, and living a champagne lifestyle from the first day. No doubt he'd hoped the business would flourish and he'd become a wealthy man in his own right."

"Poor Bartholomew," said Kate. "I'd like to know who's behind that letter getting to Inspector Ridley. That was underhand."

"Yes, but if we're to get anywhere, we must leave our feelings out of it. The letter turning up could simply be a good Samaritan giving justice a shove in the right direction."

"True, Bartholomew might actually be guilty, but I draw the line at sneaking around in other people's rooms."

"Whether Barty's guilty or not, somebody's actively responding to events. The letter makes him look the obvious suspect, just as the note made Cook look the obvious suspect. And one thing we do know – whoever wrote the note is either the killer or someone who's protecting them. Can we say the same about whoever stole the letter?"

"I wish I knew," said Kate. "It's fair to say Bartholomew's reaction to Edward's New York plans might have indicated the rejection of an earlier plan. It's not a great leap for someone to look for evidence of it in his room."

Jane considered it.

"We've been through all the suspects and their possible motives. We've also looked at who had the opportunity to commit the crime."

"All to no avail, unfortunately. The only one with an alibi is Sir Charles."

"Yes, but this time we really do need to identify the murderer. If we don't, an innocent person might hang."

"I know, Jane."

"So, how about we call this hidden character something like… X."

"X?"

"Yes, let's say that X had something to gain from Edward's death."

"Go on."

"Well, what if X wants to make sure they're not caught? Why not write a note to Cook that would guarantee she went to see Edward."

"That would mean X knew the true War story."

"Yes, but what if the finger of justice pointing at Cook begins to waver?"

"That might make X worry about coming under suspicion."

"Yes, at which point X follows a similar *modus operandi* in having a document reach the hands of the police, this time incriminating Bartholomew Grantley."

"Hmm," said Kate, "I really don't like the sound of X."

"If there *is* an X at work, we need to act fast – before too many of us leave Linton Hall."

"I agree. We should assume there really is an X. If we're wrong, it won't matter, but if we're right…"

"We could save an innocent person from the gallows."

"So, who might be X…? Oliver?"

"Possibly," said Jane. "He had a strong motive for killing Edward."

"What about Timothy Lawson?"

"If he was blackmailing Edward, why kill him?"

"Hmm. And what of Victoria and Charlotte working together? If they had a joint motive, they'd be false alibis for each other."

"It's possible."

"Then there's Margaret."

"She was playing piano," said Jane. "Leaving the music room wasn't beyond her. But what would she gain?"

"Pritchard?" Kate ventured.

"I know he was the last to see Edward alive, but I just don't see it."

Kate went to the door to check the hallway again. She then came back.

"If I were to go with instinct, I'd still say Timothy Lawson is our man. He's awful."

"I agree he's no charmer," said Jane, "but that doesn't mean he's a murderer. Of course, if there were a secret motive…"

"Yes, the motive's still the thing."

"Then that's our task," said Jane. "To look harder."

"Let's go upstairs. Perhaps we'll have a few final thoughts before bed."

They headed down the hallway, where Florence appeared up ahead, coming out of the living room.

"Oh, hello," she said.

"Jane and I wanted to go over a few ideas quietly," said Kate. "It hasn't come to much though."

"It's the same in there," said Florence as the three of them made for the stairs. "Charlotte, Timothy and Victoria are currently disagreeing with Margaret, Oliver and Sir Charles. Frankly, I was getting a headache from all the speculation."

At the top of the stairs, Kate and Jane bade Florence good night.

"Let's set aside those with obvious motives," Jane whispered as they made their way to their rooms. "That's Florence and Pritchard worrying about saving the roof over their head, and Oliver, who stood to gain the title and the estate. We can also set aside, just for now, Barty, whose motive we know."

"Charlotte had a clear motive," said Kate. "She's reliant on funding for her lifestyle, whatever that happens to be."

"Possibly," said Jane.

By now, they had reached Kate's door.

"Could she really be working with Victoria?" Kate wondered. "A joint motive we're unaware of?"

"We need to investigate further, Aunt."

"Yes, but how?"

"Everyone's downstairs…"

*

Jane calmly entered Charlotte's room on the family's landing and switched the light on.

"I'll keep cavey," whispered Kate.

It struck her that it was a phrase she hadn't used since school. Keep cavey, to keep watch… in case a teacher came along while mischief was underway. Yes, she missed those far off days. Latin had been a favourite. *Cave…* beware, watch out. Where had the time gone since she last kept cavey?

"The array of wool here," said Jane. "Both bold and subtle dyed colours. And inventive patterns. She's very creative."

"I do enjoy knitting," said Kate, trying to take her mind off the fact that she was now a burglar's accomplice. "I can spend hours losing myself in a long winter scarf."

A couple of minutes later, Jane stepped out of the room and quietly closed the door.

"There's nothing I can find. Let's try Victoria's room while there's time."

She was soon inside, while Kate stood at the door wondering why each passing second felt like ten.

Initially, it seemed a lost cause.

But then, in a drawer beneath some underwear…

"A diary," Jane reported.

"Perhaps we shouldn't look."

"We must," Jane insisted. Indeed, she was already checking the most recent entries. "Here, two days ago she wrote, 'Oliver will be making an announcement. At last!' That's with an exclamation."

"Interesting," said Kate. "Florence mentioned something about an announcement. I wonder why it's in Victoria's diary."

Jane left the room.

"What about Timothy Lawson?" said Kate, even though the idea made her feel uneasy.

Jane looked less than enthusiastic. But only for a moment.

"Yes, we should."

She slipped inside his room while Kate remained at the door. There was a case under the bed. Jane dragged it out and tried the catch.

"Locked. I dare say he keeps the key in his pocket."

"Jane, someone's coming."

"Right, take a step inside, Aunt."

Kate stepped across the threshold and stood facing into the room. She hoped the pounding in her chest wasn't an indicator of a final few seconds before her heart packed up, because it certainly felt like it.

Jane came to stand beside her.

"Very strange," she said loudly.

"What is?" Timothy demanded before coming to a halt

at the threshold.

"Your door," said Jane. "It's wide open."

That's true, thought Kate.

Especially after we opened it.

"What's going on?" Timothy insisted.

"It was dark inside," said Jane, very calmly. "We thought for a moment someone had perhaps gone in and fallen over."

"Precisely," said Kate, trying to mask her unease.

"But all's well," said Jane.

"What about my door?"

Kate sighed. "It's a question that may never be answered."

A moment later, they were in Kate's room.

"Well done, Jane," she said, her heart still thumping a little. "That took some nerve."

"It a shame we didn't learn a bit more."

"I know. But this announcement business. I think we should see Florrie."

"In the morning?" Jane assumed.

"No, now."

Without delay, they were at Florence's door giving a light knock. She was surprised to find them outside when she opened it.

"What is it?"

"A private matter," said Kate.

"Couldn't it wait?"

"No."

"You'd better come in then."

Once inside, Kate reported the entry in Victoria's diary.

To say the least, Florence wasn't happy.

"That's appalling. You can't go around peeking into people's diaries."

Kate wasn't having it.

"Florrie, someone is going around trying to get people hanged for murder. A diary cannot be allowed to get in the way of justice."

"Quite so," said Jane. "Now, the other day, you mentioned an announcement."

"Yes, well, from the diary entry, it's clear that Victoria's expecting Oliver to announce their engagement."

"Is that so?" said Kate.

"Yes," said Florence, "but here's the thing…"

Twenty-Eight

Kate and Jane were soon back in Kate's room, the elder sitting on the edge of the bed, the younger standing by the window. They were already analysing the case against Victoria Eustace.

"Imagine her state of mind," said Jane. "Oliver had come to a decision about announcing their engagement but was then unable to act on it due to his father's death. However, events were about to take a couple of disturbing turns."

"Edward's murder," said Kate.

"Yes, Edward's murder, but more significantly, Oliver being suspected of the crime. Under those circumstances, might Victoria attempt to save her secret fiancé from the gallows?"

"The way you present the case, Jane, it's entirely possible."

"It's only a theory, but someone stole a letter from Bartholomew that incriminates him. It could well be Victoria getting Oliver off the hook."

"Possibly, but it's not proof. We could equally say Timothy Lawson might be the letter thief. He knew about the dealings between Barty and Edward."

"Yes, he did," said Jane, "but I don't think he gained from Edward's death."

"Hmm… that doesn't help us much then."

Kate stared into the remains of the fire and felt a little lost.

"To think we were sneaking around in other people's rooms for nothing. All that whispering, tippy-toeing, quietly opening and closing doors…"

Just then, something clicked in Kate's mind.

"Jane… something's just come back to me."

"What is it?"

"With all that's gone on… the murder, the shock, the investigation, the brain-wracking… my head's been so full of conspiracies and conundrums that… well, it's about Timothy and Edward arguing."

"Go on…"

Kate wrestled with it.

"Oh, I'm not sure. I think it's fatigue. Whatever we come up with, nothing establishes anyone's guilt."

"Take a moment, Aunt. Let your mind clear."

"Yes, well… it's all that sneaking about. It's triggered a memory. On the guests' landing… I think someone was at their door while Edward and Timothy were arguing. And they would have heard more than I did."

"Any idea who?"

Kate thought for a moment.

"I'm not sure."

"I was in my room," said Jane. "I never heard a thing."

"No, well, with the depth of these rooms, and the thickness of the doors… to listen to whispered voices on the landing, you'd need to be standing right by an open door."

Jane considered it.

"Yet another person who may or may not know the true War story. It doesn't change things though. If we're to get to the bottom of it, we're going to need a clear-cut, decisive breakthrough. Otherwise…"

"…a jury could be persuaded to find Bartholomew guilty?"

Jane began pacing between the door and the window.

"What did Victoria say? It's the way of the world. Barty needed Edward for his name. Barty himself is a good businessman but he had no way to move in the circles he did."

Kate nodded. "She also said his mother married above her station. Poor Barty. I don't like to hear things like that. I believe it's right that young people with talent should be free to rise above their so-called betters. Men like Barty risked their lives for this country during the War. They deserve more than to be sneered at by the likes of Victoria Eustace and Timothy Lawson."

"Mind you, Timothy seemed to hate Edward more than he does Barty. He at least had the decency to acknowledge Barty as the brains."

Kate rubbed her eyes and stifled a yawn.

"So, who's the murderer? Cook? Barty? Timothy? Oliver? Margaret? Or Victoria and Charlotte working together?"

"There's something missing," said Jane. "Something we've overlooked. I'm sure of it. Let's return to the core issue. This was all about Edward."

"Yes, but I'm not sure how that helps us solve the case or, indeed, stay awake."

"What do we know about him? He returned home from the War but couldn't settle. A year or two later, he went to live in Paris where he became an art dealer, possibly a bad one."

"He also drank too much, Jane."

"It's not uncommon for alcohol to fuel rash decisions. He also struck me as someone lacking the patience to learn his subject in depth. That's another direct route to misjudgement."

"Absolutely."

"Now we suspect he returned to England three months ago because Barty was setting up the London operation. But let's go back a little. He made a few visits home over the years. I'd suggest he wanted to keep in with his father.

It may be his allowance was the only thing funding his chosen lifestyle."

"Oh Jane, to think George asked me to arrange an introduction. I'm worried now it was simply to hand Edward a new source of income."

"I think we're safe on that score, Aunt. Now let's think about Paris a little more. Charlotte became friends with Victoria and took her there to look at fashion and art. While there, Charlotte became entranced by the Bohemian lifestyle. Now Victoria insists she only met Edward briefly, but do we believe she had no interest in getting to know the heir to the Linton estate?"

Kate gave it some thought.

"Perhaps it was Edward who wasn't interested in Victoria."

"Well, he wasn't a generous man. He wouldn't have been captivated by a woman of limited means."

"Oh, I'm sure Victoria's quite well off."

"Think about it, Aunt. She made a point of mentioning a Paris haute couture fashion show at Barker's of Kensington, but the shape of the dress in question is just a little off. I doubt she bought it there."

"Ah now, you're wrong there, Jane. She specifically said she did."

"No, Aunt Kate. She did not."

"Didn't she? My ears must need testing."

"If I recall correctly, Victoria said, 'I paid a visit to Barker's of Kensington. They held a fashion show there.

Exclusive Paris haute couture.' She never said that's where she bought the dress."

"Goodness me. You're right."

"She also said something about designs by Chanel and others being incredibly expensive, but that it opens one's eyes."

"Ah, you mean it might open one's eyes to a more expensive lifestyle."

"Yes."

"So, you don't think she's comfortably off then?"

"Have you noticed how her perfume quickly fades to nothing? No, I don't think she's comfortably off, although it's important we believe she is."

"Interesting," said Kate. "And of course Charlotte paid for them both to go to Paris. If Victoria's a woman of means, that would seem unnecessary."

"Yes, Paris, where Victoria first met Edward. When I asked about the second time she met him, she seemed surprised. Even caught off-guard."

"Ah, but they only saw him once in Paris. It was at a gallery."

"She chooses her words carefully. She said *we* saw him just the one time at the gallery. It's no indicator of how many times she saw him by herself."

"Oh… I see."

"I believe Victoria saw Edward again. I also believe he had no interest in her. That brings us back to Victoria's friendship with Charlotte. Despite them having nothing whatsoever in common, Victoria has remained a close friend to Charlotte, who has another brother in Oliver. I say that, because I've yet to witness a single ray of warmth pass from Victoria to Charlotte. Not a piece of gossip, a shared joke, a reminder of past escapades. Nothing. As far as their friendship goes, they may as well be two strangers sitting together on a train."

"But what does it mean for our investigation?"

"There's something there, Aunt... just out of reach. Oh, what are we missing?"

"I wish I knew."

"Let's quieten our minds for a moment. Something might come to us."

"Good idea," said Kate – although her silence failed to last. "Ooh, there's such a chill in the air. Is that window properly closed?"

Jane smiled and peeked behind the curtain.

"It couldn't be shut any tighter."

"The weather's turning colder, Jane. No doubt about it."

"We're not back to Mount Everest, are we?"

"No, although it's fair to say I've known genuine cold weather."

"But not on Everest."

"No, but almost as challenging. I once spent three winter weeks in Scotland, and I can tell you it was absolutely freezing. Have you ever been up there in winter?"

"Yes, but let's try again to quieten our minds. Something might yet come to us."

Jane sat down on the edge of the bed beside her aunt, and for a moment there was complete silence. But once again, it failed to last, as Kate was soon up – and now it was she who was pacing the floor.

"Timothy Lawson," she said. "He knew the War story and he knew of the dealings between Bartholomew and Edward. I'm sure of it, Jane. It was Timothy."

"You're overlooking something important, Aunt."

"Am I?"

"Timothy told the true War story to Barty and Sir Charles. The question that's been bothering me is why?"

"Now you mention it, yes, why?"

"I need to think about it a bit more, but if I'm right, it could let Timothy off."

Kate retrieved the poker from the fireside stand and tried to agitate some life into the dying embers.

"No, Timothy's exactly the type to steal that letter and write the note to Cook. I'd say he stood to lose his role as the Lintons' financial advisor and it tipped him over the edge."

She replaced the poker and turned to address her audience directly.

"Wouldn't you agree he's ruthless?"

Jane's eyes widened. She seemed to be in the grip of something.

"Jane? Are you alright?"

"Oh, Aunt Kate, I'm such a fool!"

"I'm sure you're not."

"But I am. I've not been thinking straight."

"How do you mean?"

"It's something you said… something I couldn't see…"

"About Timothy being the type to write the note?"

"No, you mentioned the cold weather."

"Um… I don't quite…?"

"The cold weather. I can't believe I overlooked it!"

"Right, so… the cold weather… hang on, it brought Bartholomew back from the river early. Are you saying *he's* the killer?"

"Aunt, it's time for a little excursion outside."

"At midnight?"

"Yes, we're going to the Red Lion!"

Twenty-Nine

Jane brought Gertie to a halt with a gentle squeak of the brakes. It was past midnight, it was frosty, and they were outside the Red Lion pub. Worse still, Kate didn't approve of breath that formed a frozen mist in front of her face.

"Hopefully, he hasn't gone to bed," she said. "Then again, it's a pub. If he's still up, he could be roaring drunk."

"Aunt, really. He's an inspector from Scotland Yard. I'm sure he's had an early night."

They got out of the car and approached one of the Red Lion's front windows. The interior was dark.

"We'll have to wake up the whole pub," Kate surmised.

She began thumping her fist on the door.

"We might succeed in waking up the whole village," Jane pointed out as the noise reverberated along the street.

But any further observations were cut short by the sound of an upstairs sash window opening.

"Who's there?" came a male voice streaked with annoyance.

"Mrs Forbes and Lady Jane Scott."

"I'm full up. If one of you is a genuine ladyship, try Linton Hall. Goodnight!"

"No, don't go. We're here to see Inspector Ridley."

The window had almost closed on them, but it grudgingly opened once more.

"What's this about? You can't come around here waking people up at night. Inspector or no inspector."

Kate bristled. "There have been developments in a murder case. Am I to say the landlord of the Red Lion helped or hindered justice? You might want to consider that for when your license next comes up."

"Oh, wait there."

The window slammed shut and Kate tutted.

"Where else does he think we'd wait?"

A couple of minutes later, lights came on downstairs followed by the sound of bolts being drawn. Finally, the door opened to reveal an elderly balding man in a dark dressing gown.

"At last," said Kate. "Any longer and you'd have found two frozen corpses on the doorstep."

"I've banged on Ridley's door and told him you're here. Mrs Fraud and Lady Despot, wasn't it?"

"Mrs Forbes and Lady Jane Scott. What did the inspector say?"

"I wouldn't like to repeat it, madam."

"Yes, well, I assume he's coming down. How about we step inside?"

"If you insist."

He held the door open for them.

A few moments later, they were seated at a bare wooden table amid an odour of stale beer.

"So, is this Grantley bloke really the murderer?" the landlord asked.

"That's a police matter," Kate advised him. "It's all dealt with in the strictest confidence."

"Oh right, only the regulars in tonight were exchanging two-to-one bets on it being the brother."

"I don't approve of gambling. And I'm hoping it wasn't Oliver Linton."

"Me too. I've got money on the sister."

Just then, heavy footsteps could be heard on a flight of hidden stairs… and a moment later, from somewhere behind the bar, Inspector Ridley emerged.

"Right, what's going on?" he grumbled. "I don't know if to listen to you or charge you both with a breach of the peace."

"It's alright, inspector," said the landlord. "Mrs Forks and Lady Jam Pot are going to give us the latest on the murder case. Turns out it might yet be the sister."

"Yes, if you wouldn't mind leaving us," said Ridley. "This is police business."

"Well, you could've fooled me," the landlord huffed before grudgingly making his way back upstairs.

"Now, what's all this about?" Ridley demanded.

"Jane's worked it out," said Kate. "At least, she might have."

"We think we know the murderer's identity," said Jane. "The problem lies in proving it."

"Alright, let's hear it then. As quick as you like."

"Well…" Jane began. "The cold weather put me on the right path."

"The cold weather?" said Ridley. "That was Grantley's excuse for returning to the house early. Are you confirming he's the killer? Only, I still have a nagging doubt about that. Unless you're saying it left Oliver Linton on his own…"

"Just allow me a moment to explain," said Jane, "then I'll give you the name of the killer, the motive, and the reason why detection has proven so difficult."

"Are you sure? Only, this entire investigation is like a boxing match where we can't land any blows. What I need is a knockout punch. Unfortunately, it's the one thing I lack."

"You want a knockout punch?" said Jane.

"Yes, I do. A great big knockout punch. One the killer won't get up from."

"Alright, I'll hand you one."

"You will?"

"Yes," said Jane. "Knitting."

"What?"

Kate sighed. "She said knitting."

"I heard what she said."

"Good," said Kate. "Now let Jane explain it, then we can all sleep on it. Tomorrow morning, if you think she's right, we can all gather at Linton Hall. Shall we say, ten o'clock?"

Thirty

At ten o'clock on a bright Christmas Eve morning, Kate and Jane were in the library. It was once again a peaceful place to sit quietly, whether reading, writing or simply contemplating.

As it was, Kate was leafing through a biography of an East India Company man she had never heard of who visited places she had also never heard of.

Jane meanwhile stood at the window, which, like the study, afforded a view over the drive.

"I wonder where the Malacca Straights are," Kate mused.

"British Malaya, I believe," said Jane.

Kate turned the page with little interest in the contents.

"I don't think it was a good idea to let everyone know you've worked out the killer's identity. They've since been acting strangely. They *all* look like killers."

"Do you think he'll come?" Jane asked.

She sounded doubtful.

Kate sighed and put the book down.

"I don't know, Jane. What I do know is that we've made more progress than we thought possible. If Inspector Ridley chooses to reject your breakthrough, that's his business. Do you know it reminds me of a theft case my husband passed sentence on. He sent a man to prison for two years. Six months later, evidence came to light that proved his innocence – evidence the police had originally dismissed as unimportant."

"Six months might be too late in a murder case."

"Well, I suppose sometimes we just have to take a breath and tell ourselves we did our best. For you, Jane, I'd suggest studying extra history to take your mind off it. The Rise and Fall of the Roman Empire should keep you busy for a few months…"

"Sorry to change the subject, Aunt Kate, but there's a police car coming up the drive."

*

Kate and Jane greeted a dour Inspector Ridley at the front door.

"Morning," he grumbled.

"Well?" said Kate.

"I'm agreeing to this, but I can't say I'm happy about it. I don't make a habit of allowing amateurs to take charge of an investigation."

Kate bristled.

"Inspector Ridley, you have in your pocket a handwritten note to Cook whose authorship has proven impossible to determine. You also have a letter of Bartholomew Grantley's that was made available to you by an unknown hand. If you're unhappy about anything, it should be the possibility of the wrong person facing the death penalty, and not that an amateur might solve the case."

"Yes, well… let's get this over and done with. I'll have everyone gathered in the living room. You can address them there."

"Me?" said Kate, shaking her head. "No, we need someone with a firm grasp of the ins and outs of it. Jane, obviously."

"Me?" said Jane, a little taken aback.

"You cracked the case," said Kate. "With all those strands, I'd end up in a tangle."

It took a moment, but Jane soon recovered her composure.

"If you're sure," she said.

"I am."

"Right, well… the living room. Actually, inspector, would you mind if we gathered in the blue drawing room instead?"

"Yes, alright," said Ridley, somewhat irritably, "but remember, I'm leaving in twenty minutes to catch a train back to London."

"Yes, of course," said Jane. "If you wouldn't mind spending a couple of those minutes waiting here first."

"What for?"

"I'd like you and I to have a private word with Lord Oliver Linton. Whatever he hears in that room, he must remain silent. A life may depend on it."

Thirty-One

As requested, everyone had gathered in the blue drawing room where, predictably, there was a general muttering about the situation.

"I'm getting a little tired of this," Charlotte Linton was heard to remark above all other voices. "Isn't the man responsible for Edward's death in a police cell?"

Nevertheless, while Ridley remained by the door, Jane moved across the room to the fireplace without acknowledging anyone's concerns.

"Have they put you in charge?" Sir Charles Sutton asked as she turned to face them.

"Absolutely not," said Jane. "I've simply been given permission to make a few observations."

"Yes," said Ridley, "so if we could all remain quiet, it would be much appreciated."

"Thank you, inspector," said Jane. "I'd like to begin with Edward, the eighth baron. He was hardly a popular figure, but what happened here had little to do with popularity."

Timothy Lawson, sitting by the table, stirred.

"Is it your intention to name the killer, Lady Jane? Only, Charlotte's right. The police already have their man."

"All in good time, Mr Lawson. Now let's consider the victim drinking heavily at lunch."

"Not for the first time," muttered Florence. "His father didn't approve, you know. It started during the War."

"Yes," continued Jane. "Now, Edward went to the library to sleep it off. We know he didn't like to show his weakness, and that sleeping it off in bed would only confirm that weakness."

"Hence the library sham," said Sir Charles.

"Yes," said Jane, "but knowing he'd be vulnerable isn't enough. The killer also had to know the true story of Reginald Parker's fate and, most importantly of all, be in a position to gain from Edward's death. Now, regarding the War story, only Mr Lawson, Mr Grantley and Sir Charles knew it for certain."

"Sir Charles has an alibi," said Florence.

"A whole pub full of alibis," Sir Charles added.

"Yes... there's also the possibility that Oliver and Charlotte knew the story. After all, Edward was their brother. He might have told them. Then there's Cook. Someone might have told her long ago of her son's true fate."

Jane paused for a moment to take stock.

"Last night, something was bothering Aunt Kate. She wasn't sure at first, but she became more and more certain that someone on the guests' landing was at their door during Timothy and Edward's argument. By a process of elimination, based on who was where at the time, it could only have been one of Victoria or Margaret."

Florence stirred but stopped short of speaking.

"It's just more names," said Charlotte.

"Yes, we have quite a few in all," said Jane. "And among them, we'll find one who is not only callous enough to take a life, but also willing to see an innocent party take the blame and hang for it."

"I trust this isn't about to fall on me," said Timothy. "I certainly didn't kill him."

"I believe you," said Jane. "No blackmailer would kill off a valuable source of income."

There were several gasps.

"What?" said Timothy. "How dare you!"

"The problem was Edward declining to pay up, which is why you were arguing. His defence would have been to insist he didn't care if you told anyone. Sending a common soldier for brandy on the front line? Arrogant, entitled Edward Linton saw nothing wrong with it. But you knew the idea of Edward not caring about his reputation to be a lie. After all, here was a man who pretended to read in the library when he was drunk. No, Edward cared about his reputation and so remained a viable target. It just required a little more work on your part. That's why you told Barty and Sir Charles the true War story – to scare Edward by showing you meant business. Who would you tell next? He'd have to pay up to stop you."

Timothy stood up.

"Very clever, Lady Jane, but—"

"Oh, sit down!" growled Sir Charles. "And stop denying you're a blackmailer."

"What?"

"You were all fussing over my whereabouts that lunchtime. Yes, I was in the Red Lion. But before that, I spent some time with Edward."

"Oh?" said Timothy.

"Everything Lady Jane says is true. The thing she doesn't know is that you were originally extorting money from his father. The one thing dear old George couldn't abide was the reality that, following Alistair's death, the new heir was a drunk and a coward. Hence him paying you an inflated fee for your never-ending financial services."

"That's not blackmail."

"It's as good as," said Sir Charles, now emphasising each word by jabbing the thin end of his pipe towards Timothy. "You're nothing more than a crook."

"I knew it!" said Kate.

"Alright, that's enough," said Ridley. "I might look into that later. Lady Jane, please continue."

"Thank you, inspector. Now, I'd like to take us in a different direction. The cold weather."

A look of confusion spread across most faces.

"Last night, my aunt mentioned the chill in the air. For a moment I wondered if she might benefit from having another scarf. That thought then led me to the business of knitting, which in turn made me think about the murder in a different way."

"Did you say knitting?" Florence asked.

"Yes, Mrs Nettleton, the clickety-clack of needles making use of wool. When Aunt Kate and I left Charlotte and Victoria that fateful lunchtime, Victoria's was the only knitting bundle in this room."

"I can vouch for that," said Kate. "I sat on it."

"Fortunately, my beloved aunt was unharmed."

Charlotte piped up. "I hope you don't think I had anything to do with my brother's death?"

"When Margaret and I walked down to the music room, we followed you and Victoria. You came in here to play chess."

"Which we did," said Charlotte.

"Yes, except in your statement, you said you both played chess and did some knitting. Victoria's statement corroborates this. She says exactly the same thing."

"That's because it's true."

"So, Charlotte's the killer?" said Sir Charles. "Not for money, I hope, my dear."

"I'm no killer!" Charlotte protested.

Jane pushed on. "Charlotte, where did you sit when you played chess?"

Charlotte took a moment to calm down.

"Just there, where Mr Lawson's sitting."

Timothy Lawson looked ready to dart from the chair, but Jane had more to say.

"Just as I thought. It makes the most sense."

"Is that the proof?" Timothy asked.

"Let's not leap too far ahead," said Jane. "What we know for certain is that only Victoria's knitting bundle was here when they came in. Therefore, at some point, Charlotte left the room. Now, the maid was in Arundel with the footman, but had she been available, I doubt Charlotte would trust a servant to get her things."

"I'm creative," said Charlotte. "I'd never send the maid to choose patterns or colours. But you're forgetting something. Although I went for my things, I returned before Pritchard took Edward the coffee."

"And at what time did Pritchard carry out that duty?"

"Half past two."

"How do you know it was half past two?"

"It may have escaped your detective powers, Lady Jane, but that's the time Pritchard says he entered the library."

"Quite right, Charlotte. Very well…"

"Sorry to interrupt," said Ridley. "But that confirms Charlotte Linton was in this room with Victoria Eustace at the time of the murder."

"And what time was the murder, inspector?" Jane asked.

"Between half past two and when the body was discovered at ten to three."

"Fine. By the way, what's the time now?"

Jane was standing beside the mantlepiece clock, inviting Ridley to read it.

"Twenty-five past ten, obviously."

"Are you sure?"

"What?" Ridley delved into his waistcoat for his fob watch. Others consulted their own timepieces.

"Hang on," said Ridley. "That clock's ten minutes slow."

"Allow me to set it right for you," said Jane.

She reset the minute hand to the correct time and gazed at Charlotte.

"Not checking your watch, Charlotte? Oh, pardon me. You don't wear one, or for that matter, any other adornments beyond your beads of tranquillity. You'd have to trust this clock, wouldn't you."

Jane turned to Ridley.

"Would you trust this clock, inspector? If a life depended on it?"

Ridley tucked his fob watch away.

"Please do continue," he said.

Thirty-Two

While Lady Jane looked around the blue drawing room, no doubt gathering her thoughts, Kate was praying her niece would soon pull all the strings together without faltering.

"This is all very interesting," said Charlotte, "but for some odd reason, you're wilfully overlooking Barty."

"That's because he's not the killer," said Jane. "If he were, we wouldn't be gathered here."

Victoria shrugged. "He lied to the police twice and then ran."

"Yes, he did. He was scared. He had no alibi. And worse, the real killer presented that letter to Inspector Ridley. By then, Barty could hardly talk his way out of it with an apology. Let's be clear, miscarriages of justice do happen. They're real."

Jane left the thought there for a moment before continuing.

"Bartholomew was the smartest business brain under this roof. Even Timothy Lawson is gracious enough to recognize it. No, what happened that terrible afternoon was carried out by a calculating mind willing to risk their life to gain everything they were obsessed with. But that's not Barty. He was knocked down, but he has the wits to dust himself off and have another go."

"It's true that Barty has a bright future," said Timothy.

"Let's get back onto the trail of the killer," said Jane. "Perhaps you can help me further, Mr Lawson. Are you able to see the library door from where you're sitting?"

"What?"

"The library door?"

Timothy reluctantly craned his neck past Inspector Ridley towards the open door.

"No," he said. "I can't even see into the hallway."

"I'd also suggest that with the radio on, anyone sitting there wouldn't have heard Pritchard come along either. Just one final question for you then. You've turned your chair around to face me. But if you were facing the table to play chess, would you be able to see the clock?"

"No, just my opponent and the wall behind."

"Good. Now, if you could all bear with me just a little longer, I'll tell you what I believe took place in this house."

Kate noted Jane looking across to Inspector Ridley. Perhaps she was thinking of the train he intended to catch. That said, he seemed in no hurry. Indeed, he nodded to her.

Jane took a steadying breath.

"Now… I want everyone to imagine that afternoon as if it were happening right now. I want you to be a ghostly presence, an unseen observer, free to move around as events unfold."

"Do we have to play such a silly game?" said Victoria.

But Jane ignored her.

"Imagine… Miss Victoria Eustace sitting at the table opposite Mr Lawson's seat. Imagine… while playing chess, she sees Pritchard taking the coffee to Edward, and then watches him leave again. Suddenly, an idea manifests itself. It's a dazzling notion, far more daring than any complicated chess strategy, but it would give Victoria everything she desires. All she need do is keep her nerve for a few minutes. Observe… as she studies the carriage clock on the mantlepiece. It shows half past two. Of course it does. That's when Pritchard serves Edward's coffee every afternoon. Watch… as she gets up from the table to stretch her legs. With Charlotte facing away from the mantlepiece, it's easy to change the time on the clock. And now it's easy to say that it's twenty minutes past two. Listen… as she suggests they switch knitting. Perhaps Charlotte could select one or two patterns she's most proud of. And Charlotte, don't forget to bring some clever colour combinations."

"She did," said Charlotte. "I've created over fifty patterns, so it took time to choose a couple."

"Charlotte's happy," Jane continued. "This is her passion. So, let's imagine further… while she's up in her room, Victoria enters the library. Whether Edward is fully asleep or just waking, she takes the ceremonial dagger and stabs him. She then wipes the handle of the blade with his top pocket handkerchief. Now, using her left hand, she writes a short note to Cook and carefully places it in an envelope without leaving fingerprints. Even Edward's pen is wiped clean. All's quiet, so she hurries down the hallway to the kitchen. Pritchard is further along, in the pantry cleaning the silver. Undetected, she slides the note under the kitchen door and hurries back to the blue drawing room."

"This is pure fantasy," said Victoria.

But Jane wasn't about to stop.

"Over by the window, the sun is blazing through. A few minutes later, as Charlotte enters, an unusually excited Victoria calls her over to where they might study the patterns and colours in the sunlight. So, Charlotte sits with her back to the door as she starts on a new cardigan, making it easy for Victoria to mention Pritchard leaving the library. The clock even shows half-past two, although it's highly doubtful Charlotte would bother to look. After all, clocks are the domain of those who work for a living. So, there they are, by the window, for as long as it takes for someone to discover the body."

"Ridiculous," muttered Victoria.

But the rest of the room was silent.

Jane meanwhile held back for a moment, perhaps gathering her strength for a final thrust.

"The next important event is the crash of the vase. Charlotte goes out to see what it was. Victoria changes the clock to the correct time and follows. It seems Edward's been murdered. Amid the chaos, Victoria is confident of success. Later, when Charlotte is questioned she says she was knitting with Victoria at half past two when Pritchard served Edward's coffee. Victoria even said, 'There goes poor Pritchard.' Of course, she said it while peering into an empty hallway because Pritchard had been and gone before Charlotte went for her knitting."

"The whole thing seems unlikely," said Charlotte.

"My aunt lost time between gongs when her watch stopped," said Jane. "That made me wonder. History teaches us there are many ways to measure time. Charlotte, when Sergeant Thompson was in charge, you mentioned how you didn't get as much knitting done as normal during that fateful period, despite your experienced hands. That's because the time between Victoria telling you that Pritchard had served the coffee and the crash of the vase wasn't twenty minutes. It was more like ten."

Charlotte frowned.

"That's… surely… actually, that would make sense."

Victoria stood, red faced.

"I had nothing to gain from Edward's death. I met him briefly in Paris, that's all. This whole business of changing the clock and writing a note… it has nothing to do with me. Anyone could have gone into the library. After I saw Pritchard, I became too engrossed in Charlotte's creations to notice what was going on elsewhere."

Jane left Victoria's words hanging for a moment before continuing.

"Charlotte, why did you go to Paris?"

"Paris? For art… and culture, but I don't see what it has to do with…"

"Was it your own idea to go?"

"No, Victoria prompted me. Her descriptions of the artistic life there made it impossible for me to stay away."

"Why didn't you go alone?"

"Victoria knew everything I needed to know. She had to come."

"So, you paid for her to go with you."

"Yes, she'd already spent her allowance on dresses by French designers, so I paid for her. I needed her with me."

"And was Victoria aware that Edward, the bachelor heir to the Linton estate, was living there?"

"Yes, of course."

"So, there you were in Paris with Victoria. Did you spend every moment together?"

"No, Victoria liked to go off by herself. She did that several times. Frankly, I was a little bored by it after a while."

"You said that you and Victoria only saw Edward the one time there. At a gallery."

"That's right."

"Except, Victoria saw him again, by herself, several times. Without making any progress though."

"This is one false accusation after another," said Victoria. "I'd remind everyone that Lady Jane has failed to provide a single shred of genuine evidence."

Jane looked directly at Victoria, who seemed to shrink back a little.

"You say you had nothing to gain from Edward's death."

"That's right. I had no motive whatsoever."

"Well, without a motive, there's no case to answer. But you *did* stand to gain from Edward's death. Very much so. As a woman secretly waiting to become engaged to Oliver Linton, you would become the wife of the ninth baron."

Kate leapt up.

"That's the motive!"

She sat down again. But none looked to either woman. All eyes were now on Oliver. He, however, said nothing, as requested by Jane.

Thirty-Three

"May I say something on Victoria's behalf," said Florence Nettleton.

Now all eyes turned in her direction.

"I've no idea if Lady Jane is right, but I just feel it's worth pointing out that Victoria is from a very good family."

"Yes, she is," said Jane. "She's proud of her family tree. Hence an interest in family history. That's why she became friends with Charlotte Linton – in order to pursue Edward Linton, heir to the Linton estate. He, alas, had no interest in a woman of limited means."

"It's all nonsense," Victoria muttered. "I'm from a wealthy family."

"There's no crime in wearing copies of original French haute couture and less than expensive perfume," said Jane. "It's certainly no indicator of a person's true worth. The problem arises when a liking to be seen as wealthy becomes an obsession. Having used Charlotte to get to Edward, you used her again to get to Oliver."

"Is this true?" said Charlotte.

"Lady Jane has no idea what she's talking about," said Victoria.

Jane barely paused.

"Victoria came to Linton Hall with no plan to kill Edward. She was here waiting for Oliver to use the occasion of his birthday to announce their engagement. But the seventh baron died, and Oliver's plans changed. He couldn't announce his engagement during a period of mourning. Victoria would have to be patient."

"I'm surprised the inspector's allowing this to continue," said Victoria.

Ridley said nothing.

"For you, Victoria, at your door, listening to an argument and learning the true War story – it was just another reason to dislike Edward. But then, the following day, Fate lent a hand. For a few golden minutes, a life-changing opportunity presented itself. Edward, prone in the library, Sir Charles in the pub, Mrs Nettleton asleep in her room, Mr Lawson playing billiards, Margaret playing piano in the music room, Pritchard serving Edward's coffee and then withdrawing to his pantry, Cook in the kitchen, the maid and footman away to Arundel to buy black, Oliver at the river, Bartholomew returning from the river early and going to his room…"

"I think we've heard enough," said Victoria.

"The other day, that last one spooked you. I said Aunt Kate and I saw Barty returning early from fishing and you leapt in. You said it was highly suspicious. At the time, I thought you were simply stating the obvious, but you were terrified he might have witnessed something. Lucky for you his only intention was to hide from Mr Lawson's mockery."

"I refute everything," said Victoria, perhaps growing a little in confidence and strength. "I can't think why I've been dragged into it."

"Perhaps so," said Jane. "Now, the drawing room door was open because it's always stuffy in here. At half past two, you saw Pritchard enter the library with the coffee and withdraw a moment later. By altering the clock, and by switching from chess to knitting, you made use of the opportunity. Charlotte believes she got her knitting things at twenty-past when it was in fact after two-thirty. While she was away, you murdered the man who stood between you and everything you hold dear. Status, respect and money. Then you sought to lay the blame at Cook's door with a note."

"Nonsense," Victoria insisted. "None of this is true."

"You are clever, no doubt. Given a chance to change your fortunes, you swiftly came up with a plan and you had the fortitude to enact it. You were quick to adapt too. When police interest in Oliver was at its greatest, an incriminating letter landed the blame squarely upon Bartholomew, who you despised because of his, in your eyes, lowly standing. However, in all this clever plotting and planning, you overlooked the most crucial detail of all – a detail that meant you risked your life for absolutely nothing."

"What detail?" asked Sir Charles.

"That when Oliver was about to announce his engagement, it wasn't to Victoria. It was to someone else."

"No!" said Victoria. "Oliver, tell them the truth."

Oliver took a breath. "I plan to marry Miss Margaret Tavistock."

The gathering emitted a collective gasp as Margaret moved across the room to be at his side.

"No!" Victoria insisted.

"My only disappointment," said Oliver, "is the necessity to announce it under these circumstances. Due to my father's passing, I had intended to delay the announcement until the spring as a mark of respect. Margaret understood entirely."

"You're mistaken," said Victoria. "You're not thinking straight."

Oliver studied her for a moment, before continuing.

"Victoria and I were friends. Yes, we did lots together, but it was at Victoria's prompting. She took me along to functions and even hinted that people in our position often become engaged. I foolishly failed to end it, thinking it best to gradually disengage. After all, she was my sister's best friend. That's my greatest regret because I now fear it led to my brother's death."

Margaret held his hand. Sir Charles patted his shoulder.

"You need me," Victoria insisted. "Not some silly girl who plays the piano horribly!"

"No, Victoria," Oliver replied. "Once I got to know you well, I felt less and less we could ever be any kind of match. I'd also grown fond of Margaret, who does *not* play the piano horribly. She's a very fine and patient teacher. And I say that from personal experience these past few months."

Margaret blushed while Jane took the reins again.

"Oliver had a difficult time, Victoria. You were an almost permanent fixture here, posing as Charlotte's best friend. It made his courtship with Margaret difficult. And yet, the awkward circumstances only drew them closer together. In some ways, you helped them fall in love."

As Oliver's gaze turned to his fiancée-to-be, Victoria grabbed a knitting needle and launched herself at him. The strike at his neck was true and deadly... but was deflected by the hand of Sir Charles Sutton.

As Inspector Ridley, Timothy Lawson and a constable rushed to restrain her, Victoria let rip.

"I'm better than you, Oliver Linton. I'm better than all your pathetic family. I hated Edward and I hate you! I should've killed you both!"

Finally, despite flailing arms and legs, she was subdued.

"Miss Victoria Eustace," said a slightly breathless Ridley, "I'm arresting you for the murder of Lord Edward Linton. Take her away, constable."

As Charlotte and Jane hurried to assist Sir Charles with first aid, Victoria was hauled noisily away to a waiting police wagon. Kate meanwhile turned to Florence and gave her old friend a hug.

It was over.

Thirty-Four

Kate and Jane were in the foyer, waiting to bid Inspector Ridley farewell. He, however, was busy in the hallway with Lord Oliver Linton, no doubt reassuring him that any suspicion arising during the investigation was purely professional.

Kate glanced up at the shield over the fireplace bearing the family's coat of arms and motto: *vires in unitate* – strength in unity.

"Do you think Oliver, Margaret and Charlotte might work together to make that a reality?" she said, pointing at the shield.

Jane looked up and smiled.

"Yes, I'm sure of it."

Just then, Ridley came through to the foyer followed by Oliver.

"Sir Charles is chatting away again," said Oliver. "So, no lasting damage."

"Thank goodness," said Kate.

"And the inspector telephoned the police station. Barty's being released as we speak."

"Marvellous," Kate added.

"Yes, congratulations are in order, Lady Jane," said Ridley. "That was fine detective work."

"Thanks for playing along, inspector."

Kate turned to Ridley. "Who'd have thought both you and I would be barking up the wrong tree."

"It was an awkward business," said Jane, smoothing things over. "A little luck was needed to solve it."

"You're too kind," said Ridley. "Amateurs usually rely on intuition, but not you."

"Intuition?" questioned Jane. "A wise man once said it's not a bad place to start."

Kate smiled.

"I can't argue with that," said Ridley.

"Victoria almost got away with it," said Oliver. "Barty might've been hanged."

"I don't think that troubled her," said Ridley. "In her poisonous mind, lowly Bartholomew would hang, and then some months later, you'd announce the engagement."

"What a thought."

"Inspector?" said Kate. "You know, should you ever find yourself stumped again…"

"That's very generous, Mrs Forbes… Lady Jane… but I'm sure it won't be necessary. Now, if that's all, I'll wish you a good day."

"Yes, a good day and a Merry Christmas, Inspector Ridley," said Kate with a broad smile.

"Yes, of course, I'd almost forgotten. Merry Christmas and a Happy New Year to you all."

"Let me see you to the car," said Oliver.

As they departed, Kate gave a little shrug.

"It's a pity Timothy Lawson didn't get his comeuppance. Blackmail, indeed."

"Yes, but with both George and Edward gone, there's little in the way of evidence. That said, the business of financial advice is built on reputation. Perhaps Mr Lawson's name will soon be mud, especially at Hatchborne's in the City, where he was teaching none other than Oliver Linton."

"Good," said Kate. "On the other hand, I do believe Barty will rise again."

"Yes, hopefully, next time he'll concentrate on the strength of his business plans rather than getting less-worthy men to play the trojan horse."

"Let's hope so." But Kate's mind was moving on. "Jane, I brought you here for an introduction to Edward. All that's behind us now. I suppose we ought to make our way home."

Oliver returned and no doubt overheard.

"Mrs Forbes. You *are* staying on for Christmas? Your spirit would lift us all. And Lady Jane? Could you be persuaded?"

Kate was hopeful, but also a little uncertain.

"It's a fine idea, but I think Jane might need to return home."

Jane laughed. "Oliver, my only plan was to find a way to spend Christmas with my aunt. To do so here would be lovely."

"That's settled then," said Oliver. "We'll have Aunt Florence, Sir Charles, Charlotte and Margaret with us. I've also invited Barty Grantley to stay, if that's alright with you."

"Oh, it is," said Kate thinking it would be a wonderful opportunity for everyone to get back on an even keel.

"I also gave Cook a couple of paid weeks off, but well, blow me down, she's refused to take it. She said she wants to make sure there's a happy Christmas under this roof. What do you think of that?"

"She's quite a woman," said Jane.

As Oliver hurried off to share the news, Kate smiled.

"Thank you, Jane. I thought you might want to spend Christmas in London with all those lovely festivities."

"No, Aunt. Not at all."

Kate felt a warm glow. Since her husband's passing, a degree of loneliness had crept into her life. But here was a chance for renewal, and to keep alive for a while longer her wish to become the best aunt possible. And for that she was genuinely grateful.

"In fact," said Jane. "I've been meaning to ask. I thought I might come to stay with you at Sandham-on-Sea in the New Year. We could wrap up warm for walks along the promenade and make bubbling casseroles on your old range. How does that sound?"

"Oh Jane, that's sounds wonderful… truly wonderful," said a misty-eyed Kate Forbes. "Do you know, I'm looking forward to it already."

The End (Until Next Time…)

About this Book

It's been great fun to write this book and begin the process of creating a series featuring our 'have-a-go' duo.

One of the many enjoyable tasks involved in the writing is to gain a grasp of how people such as Kate and Lady Jane lived a hundred years ago.

Jane's passion is history but reaching the upper echelons of academia in the 1920s was by no means easy for a woman, no matter how talented.

In fact, England's first female professor was Edith Morley. She was a student at King's College, London's Ladies' Department in the 1890s and studied for an Oxford degree as an external student. In 1899, although she was placed in the first class of the Oxford English honour school, as a woman, she was denied a degree.

Despite this, she rose to become a lecturer and head of department at Reading. Indeed, in 1907, as Reading prepared for university status, it awarded professorships to all heads of departments, except Edith, the only woman. Refusing to play along, she fought for her rights and, in 1908, became the UK's first female professor.

Of course, not all history of the time is quite so momentous. In 'Murder Most English', the West Sussex police have bought a second-hand Daimler. This story actually comes from Bolton, Lancashire, where the area's first ever police car was a Daimler, believed to have been bought second hand in 1925 (and driven by a PC Norris).

Finally, the fictional Linton Hall is in West Sussex somewhere south of Arundel. The countryside thereabouts is stunning, especially around the spectacular South Downs. Well worth a visit!

If you've enjoyed spending time with Kate and Jane, please do look out for future instalments of the Lady Jane & Mrs Forbes Mysteries.

The second book is:

"The Sea View Cottage Conspiracy"

Sandham-on-Sea, England, 1928.

When Lady Jane Scott goes to stay with her aunt, Kate Forbes, they are both looking forward to relaxing strolls along the sea front, Punch and Judy shows, and delicious clotted cream teas.

However, their plans are thrown into turmoil by the disappearance of an elderly villager, the activities of certain suspicious persons, and the arrival of Inspector Ridley from Scotland Yard.

It looks like those scrumptious calories will have to wait while our daring duo tackle an international conspiracy on their doorstep.

About the Author

Firstly, who is B. D. Churston?

It's a pen name for Mark, Fiona and Mike Daydy. Mark has 25 years' experience as a TV and radio writer in the UK; Fiona has 20 years' experience as a teacher; and their grown-up son Mike is an illustrator who designs our book covers. Most importantly, we're mystery fans who enjoy working together to create these stories.

So, why B. D. Churston?

This takes us back to family holidays of the 1990s. One of our favourite places to spend a week or two was Torbay in Devon. While there, one of our regular trips was from Brixham to Dartmouth via the steam railway. For us, this would begin at Churston Station for a ride down to the Dartmouth ferry. On the train, approaching the River Dart, we would crane our necks for a peek at Greenway, the home of Agatha Christie. In 2012, a new stop was introduced at Greenway Halt for those wishing to visit the house, now owned by the National Trust.

So, back to the pen name. The initials B. D. represent Brixham to Dartmouth, while Churston was always our starting point.

Of course, Churston also features as the "C" in the "ABC Murders" featuring Hercule Poirot.

To get in touch, please visit us here:

www.churstonmysteries.com